Teeth Marks

12 Twisted Tales from America's Deep South

by Matthew Weber

Content Warning

Teeth Marks is a collection of dark fiction. The stories presented here are intended to disturb. They are likely to include death, graphic violence, profanity, sexual content and other themes and images that commonly disturb. If you can't deal with these themes in your fiction, then you should avoid this book.

Contents

Suburban Facebreaker

Framed by the soft light of the vanity mirror, Vivienne Reynolds lifted her chin, pooched out her lips, and painted them a bright firetruck red. Vivienne liked lipstick so red you could practically hear the sirens. She liked to drink two screwdrivers before lunch. She liked classic rock-and-roll, men who held the door, and gems and sequins that made her shine.

What Vivienne did not like was anyone messing with her family. At fifty-seven years young, she was far too old to put up with that sort of crap.

She checked her Michael Kors watch, then licked her finger and rubbed the scratches on its face. Two minutes to seven in the morning; almost time for the show. She walked from her bedroom to the living room window and parted the drapes the width of her fist, just enough to peer through the blinds at the Markessas's house across the street.

"Mmm-mm-mmm ... You've done messed up now, Mizz Markessa." She clucked her tongue against the roof of her mouth.

Mina Markessa and her rotten little girl would soon be leaving for work, could be any moment now. Her husband, the stuffed shirt, had left a half hour earlier with their baby. Vivienne had already seen his car pass like she did every weekday morning. That's when she had slipped over to their yard and set up the surprise, while the mom and daughter stayed busy inside with their daily routine. Now all she had to do was sit back, wait, and enjoy the fireworks. Just be patient.

No, it wasn't a very neighborly thing to do, but Vivienne's family hadn't drawn first blood.

***

"Gramma, Gramma, Gramma!" Jeannie burst through the door crying one afternoon two weeks ago.

Vivienne had dozed off to a TV show about wives who kill their husbands, when her granddaughter's sobs disturbed the peace. She sat up from the couch as the little girl bounced onto her lap, burying her face in Vivienne's breast. Vivienne stroked Jeannie's braided pigtails and asked, "Honey, what on earth is the matter?"

"Kimmy hit me with a rock!" Jeannie looked up, bleeding from her forehead. Vivienne wore a blue rhinestone-studded sweater, and the cut had left a red stain on her shoulder.

"My gosh, you're hurt! Come on, sweetheart, let's get you cleaned up."

Vivienne reached for a tissue on the end table and wiped off Jeannie's wound. The cut would likely bruise, but wasn't serious. Jeannie, though, heaved and hollered with huge hyperventilating gasps, weeping uncontrollably. "She did it, Gramma. She did it on purpose! Stupid, fat Kimmy Markessa! I hate her!"

In the bathroom, Vivienne ran cold water over a washrag and patted it over the wound. "Is this the new girl who moved across the street?"

"Yes, stupid, ugly Kimmy Markessa and her fat face!"

"Why would she throw a rock at you? Did you call her names?"

"No! I wasn't doing anything."

"Were you playing together?"

"No, I was riding my Big Wheel." Her breathing slowed as she calmed down. She quit fidgeting and sat on the toilet lid to let Vivienne continue the first aid.

"Why'd she throw the rock?"

"'Cause of some dumb cat I was chasing around. Wasn't even her cat! It's that ol' gray striped tomcat that's always comin' around. I was just playing with it, and she told me to stop, and I told her to leave me alone, and she *threw a rock at me!*" Her brow pinched down in the center and darkened her big, wet, hazel eyes.

"Well, you oughtta leave that ol' tomcat alone, but that little girl still shouldn't've thrown any rocks. Bless your heart!"

"Are you gonna tell her Momma about it?"

Vivienne thought for a moment, fuming. She didn't care much for instigating drama between neighbors, but an assault on little Jeannie simply would not stand. Under the circumstances, she didn't feel like she would be the instigator. "Why, I might just do that, sweetheart."

***

Vivienne climbed the brick steps to the red front door of the Markessa's, holding the wrought iron railing so she didn't slip in her heels and crack a knee. At the top, she knocked.

After a moment a faint shuffle came from the far side of the door, and Vivienne figured someone was peering through the peephole to see who had knocked, deciding whether or not to answer. The latch clicked and the door opened with a creak. An olive-skinned woman, at least ten years younger than Vivienne and tall with flowing black hair, stood holding the door open about a foot while cradling a swaddled baby.

"May I help you?"

Vivienne couldn't place the slightly clipped foreign accent. Learning about foreign cultures had never interested her, but the lady lacked the sugary drawl of a Southerner, and that put Vivienne on guard. Most people from around here didn't hit each other with rocks, but people from other countries … Lord only knew.

"Hello. Hi." Vivienne gave a weak wave and smiled stupidly, then bit her lip. She didn't want to drop a bomb on this lady, but something had to be said. "I'm Vivienne Reynolds. I'm your neighbor from across the street. I hate that we haven't met. I should have brought you a pie or something. I've just been running around so busy. I'm sure you know how it is with kids in the house."

Vivienne paused and waited for some cordial acknowledgement from the neighbor, who so far had only leered at her suspiciously. The lady finally nodded. "Okay. I am Mina Markessa."

"Well, Mina, I felt like I needed to say something because Jeannie, my little granddaughter who lives with me, says that your little girl hit her in the head with a rock." Vivienne tried on an ingratiating smile to sell the sour news with some sweetness, but felt her eyelid tick as she did so.

"Your little girl?" the lady asked.

"My granddaughter, yes."

"The one who was hurting the cat?"

"Hurting the—wait, what? No, uh-uh. No ma'am. Jeannie was just playing with that little cat. Never touched the dang thing. She just chases it around on her three-wheel. Nobody's hurting a cat."

"That's very mean."

"Mean? What?"

"Hurting the cat."

A swelling heat gathered on Vivienne's chest. "Look, if that cat didn't want to play with her, it would run off to wherever it came from. The only thing *mean* around here is your little girl throwing rocks at my Jeannie."

"Kimmy had to defend the cat."

"My god, are you serious? It's not even your cat!"

"That doesn't matter, right is right."

Vivienne inhaled deeply and slid her tongue across her teeth. "Are you telling me it was right for your little girl to hit mine with a rock?"

"It's right to defend animals. It's wrong to hurt them." The baby grunted and wiggled in her arms.

"Jeannie was *not* hurting an animal!"

"Kimmy told me she was."

"I think your little girl is an *animal*."

"I'm not speaking with you anymore."

"You need to get your animal on a leash!"

The lady slammed the door with a loud crack.

At that moment, Vivienne thought about getting in her Buick, driving over to the Markessa's place and trenching a huge mud pit across their lawn.

But she decided not to do that.

***

Jeannie had tears in her eyes when she stepped off the school bus the Monday after the rock-throwing incident.

"What's wrong, honey?" Vivienne asked, meeting her at the street corner.

"Her!" Jeannie cried and pointed at a plump girl in a maroon sweater and blue jeans, who walked by herself along the street some thirty feet behind them. "I hate her! She kept making fun of the knot on my head the whole way home! All the kids on the bus were laughing at me!"

Vivienne glared at Kimmy Markessa, who peered up with deep brown, implacable eyes. The girl held her gaze, and didn't flinch or look away the way Vivienne expected a child to do when faced with the ire of an elder. "I wish you'd leave Jeannie alone," Vivienne told her. "She has not done a thing to you, and you're not acting very neighborly!"

The little girl didn't budge. She just stared and gave a small, dismissive shrug of her shoulders. Then Kimmy turned, so her body angled slightly away from Vivienne and more directly at her house, and she marched onward with a smirk thinning her lips.

"You stay away from Jeannie," Vivienne warned as she passed them.

"You stop harassing my daughter!" said a voice from the left.

Vivienne turned to Mina Markessa coming up the street with long, determined strides, her chin stuck out in anger.

"If your daughter will stop bullying my granddaughter," Vivienne said, "you won't hear a peep from me."

Mina turned to her daughter, who stopped beside her and looked up at her mother. "Kimmy, have you been bullying this little girl?"

Kimmy shook her head.

"Kimmy hasn't been bullying your granddaughter." Mina's head tilted slightly in what Vivienne read as a gesture of defiance.

"She was too!" Jeannie blurted. "She was making fun of me!"

Vivienne blew a jet of hot air out her nose. This Markessa woman knew her little girl was a mean-spirited brute and simply didn't care. Either that, or the little girl ran the show, and her mother had nothing between the ears. Whatever the case, if something didn't change, Vivienne would have to take more drastic action.

"Keep your daughter away from Jeannie, or else," Vivienne said through clenched teeth, wondering how Mina Markessa would look with a black eye. Maybe two of them.

"Or else what?" Mina said.

"Or *else...*" Vivienne let the word trail off. She took Jeannie's hand and they both strutted away with heads held high.

The sun hid behind a vast carpet of clouds. A warm breeze stirred through Vivienne's teased hair as she walked toward the bus stop, sipping a glass of homemade Electric Lemonade concocted of vodka, beer and concentrated Minute Maid. She turned the corner and heard the angry shouts of a familiar young voice. She stopped and listened.

Vivienne dropped her glass into the grassy ditch beside the road and broke into a rickety gallop as fast as her kitten heels would carry her. Kimmy Markessa had Jeannie down on the asphalt with her knees pinning Jeannie's arms while the larger girl batted her about the face. Jeannie's head swiveled back and forth trying to dodge the onslaught. Kimmy cackled as she hit.

Kimmy peered up just in time to see Vivienne grab her by the collar, rip her off Jeannie, and hurl her into the drainage ditch. Vivienne hoisted Jeannie, and they gripped each other in a tight hug.

"Oh, sweetheart, are you hurt? Are you okay, honey?"

Jeannie looked up from tear-stained eyes, then glanced to her left.

Mina Markessa spun Vivienne around by the shoulder, wrenching Jeannie from her grasp.

"You *bitch*!" she snarled.

With a fiery wallop, the slap knocked Vivienne backward. She staggered and clutched her burning cheek.

"If you ever touch my daughter again, I will make you regret it!" Mina, taller and younger, stood over Vivienne and glowered. Her nostrils flared with agitated breaths, and she clutched and unclutched her fingers like weapons she wasn't ready to sheath.

Stunned, Vivienne stood speechless as Mina, still holding her gaze, stepped over to help up Kimmy, who took her mother's hand.

Vivienne didn't say a word. But something within her boiled and frothed with rage as her cheek throbbed with heat. She became utterly paralyzed by an overwhelming sense of murderous wrath. A diabolical hatred for the Markessas sluiced through her veins like hot acid. A switch had been thrown, and if she were to act out her impulse then, she would end up killing the woman right there on the street, bashing her head against the asphalt in a frenzy. She would simply be unable to control herself if she so much as moved a muscle. So, she remained very still. Vivienne stood on the street, seething and rubbing her face, as Mina and Kimmy walked home together holding hands.

They had won this round.

But this shit wasn't over.

***

Now, she waited.

Seven A.M., on the dot.

Peering through the blinds, her anticipation almost too much to bear, Vivienne watched for the moment the red door to the Markessa's house opened. Kimmy only rode the bus in the afternoons. Mina took her to school in the mornings, presumably on the way to work. They left the house every weekday within minutes of seven o'clock, and today Vivienne had made sure they were going to have a very bad morning.

The Rolling Stones jammed on the stereo. The speakers thumped with an African-like rhythm pounded out on conga drums. Vivienne poured a heavy shot of Smirnoff into her screwdriver glass, using the special blue-label stuff that runs a hundred proof, because this morning she planned to celebrate what was soon to happen.

As the Markessa's front door opened, her heart beat faster. This was the moment, and Vivienne licked her lips and tasted sweetness.

Her head bobbed to the beat as Mick Jagger introduced himself as the devil.

Mina exited first, cradling something at her chest and turning to bolt the door. With her long black hair draping down her back, she shut the door and locked it without Kimmy accompanying her.

Vivienne's mouth tightened. *Where the hell was the bully?*

As Mina faced the brick steps before her, the Markessa's baby squirmed in a bundle wrapped in her arms.

Vivienne's breath caught in her throat. The hubbie and wife must have switched their driving duties for some reason.

Woo-wooo... sang the Stones.

She shot a zooming look at those brick steps, focusing on the third one from the top. That's where she had tied a taut length of fishing line between the lower two bars of the handrail system. From this distance Vivienne could see no sign of the tripwire crossing just five inches above the tread, the one nine or ten steps from the bottom. And she knew that, even up close, Mina would never see it either.

Woo-wooo...

The neighbor took the first step with those long legs swishing through a knee-length cream skirt. Vivienne swallowed and pressed her fingers together. Mina's left foot, clad in a sensible flat, landed safely on tread number two. On her third stride, the right foot met invisible resistance.

Vivienne's fingernails dug into the backs of her hands.

Oh Jesus, please forgive me.

Mina's eyes widened. Her feet tangled beneath her as a pivot point. Her body listed, and her mouth opened wide. She had only one free arm, which windmilled in a wide arc, missing the rail. Mina floated sideways. She twisted on the descent with the baby at her breast, her back positioned for impact. The child slid above her shoulder.

With a desperate wail cut brutally short, Mina crashed down onto the jagged ledges of the bricks. The baby's face crunched against a corner. Mother and child bounced and shook and slid down the steps to the driveway.

Vivienne let the blinds snap closed. A morbid coldness fell over her, and the orange juice welled back up in her throat. She steadied herself against the window with one hand and raked the other through her hair. When she pulled it away, her palm gripped a surprisingly thick nest of strands she'd ripped from her scalp accidentally.

The baby gave a shrill howl. The little one had lived.

Oh thank God...

Back at the window, Vivienne peeked out at Mina, who rolled slowly to her knees and made a pathetic moaning noise. Vivienne had always hated the sound of grown adults crying. Mina inspected the back of her head, her hand pulling away bright red. Blood spread in a patch at the back of her white blouse. She reached for her child and screamed.

When Mina lifted the little one, its tiny arms flapping, Vivienne gagged at the sight of it. The poor thing's mouth had split wide in a vertical gash. The upper lip peeled back as two flaps of skin, a newly cleft palate. The lower jaw was a blur of red, and if the baby ever had teeth, it had them no more.

Mina gave mad, whooping shrieks as she gathered the infant and its blanket and hurried them to the car. She dove inside the back door of her Tahoe, one leg kicking outside as she stretched to wrestle with the seat belts. She clambered into the driver's door, peeled out the driveway in reverse, cut a sharp left and squealed to a stop in front of Vivienne's house.

Mina rolled the tinted window down, glaring out at Vivienne right where she stood hiding in the drapes. Along with that look came a flood of pure venom, a hatred stronger than anything

Vivienne had ever felt directed at her, its energy surging across a single focused stare.

Mina coldly declared: "I am going to kill you." But she did not scream it. She did not rave the words in an uncontrolled fit of vengeful passion. She mouthed that message at Vivienne with careful, measured deliberation, not so much a threat as an oath.

And that's what chilled Vivienne the most.

Mina drove off, and the baby's cries faded in the distance.

The Stones song came to an end.

Vivienne reached for her bottle and poured another drink. Then she sneaked across the road and retrieved the broken fishing line.

***

"Of course I didn't have anything to do with it! I can't believe you'd even suggest such a thing," Vivienne told her daughter Darlene over the phone. Her cigarette hand was shaking, and she pinched it between her knees. "Serves that bitch right, though."

"Oh, but that poor baby," Darlene said. "I mean, *damn*. Little face busted up so bad. From what you said, poor thing is liable to never look right again."

Vivienne drew air between her teeth in a reverse hiss and said, "Mmm-mm-mm. I think you're right about that, honey. Can you imagine having to nurse a baby with a stitched-up face? Lordy mercy, you talk about some sleepless nights. I'd almost feel sorry for the momma if she weren't such a terrible person. But karma's what got that woman. And of all the days to take a fall like that, it had to happen on the day she had her baby. Any other day and she'd have had her other little monster. Not sure why the switch. Maybe one of the kid's had a dentist appointment or something. They sure got one now."

"Mmm-mm-mmm," Darlene said, having long ago picked up the habit from her mom. "The Lord works in mysterious ways."

"Don't He? I'll tell you what. If that lady hadn't slapped me, I'll bet things would've turned out differently for her. I believe that firmly." Vivienne took a puff from her cigarette.

Muffled voices buzzed in the background of Darlene's phone connection. "Hold on, Mom," she said, then her voice went low as she addressed someone else. Vivienne couldn't make out the exchange. "Mom, hey, I'm sorry. I'm gonna have to go. The screws here are telling me my phone privileges already ran out."

"Those bastards."

"You're telling *me*."

"When's your next parole hearing?"

"Two weeks from tomorrow."

"Two weeks…" Vivienne repeated. "Okay, well we'll be praying for you, sweetheart. We sure do miss you."

"Thanks, Mom. I love you. Give my love to Jeannie."

"I will. Bye, hon."

"Bye, Mom."

Vivienne stubbed out the butt of her Virginia Slim into an angel-shaped ashtray.

***

Vivienne found Bill's old Smith & Wesson .38, but couldn't find any bullets. She spent the afternoon straightening the house while determined to find a box of ammo she could swear she'd seen recently. Her third husband, Bill, had been a strong advocate of home defense, and when he'd passed away two years ago, she'd sold most of his firearms for a sizable chunk of money. Vivienne had only kept the pistol, in case of situations exactly like this one, because it was small, lightweight and had a manageable kick.

The search turned up nothing. A lot of good the gun would do. She took a break on the couch, the vodka caught up with her, and she woke up at quarter past nine at night. Jeannie snoozed on the sofa at her feet. The TV played an *Andy Griffith Show* rerun at low volume.

Head foggy from booze and the day's rush of excitement, Vivienne sat up and rubbed her eyes. A nip in the air raised gooseflesh on her skin. She rubbed her arms. Time to crank up the furnace.

Never before had the notion of living alone with Jeannie rattled her nerves, but the lamp beside her was the only light fixture currently on in the house, and all the dark corners at her periphery looked especially suspicious at the moment. Vivienne took the unloaded .38 from the end table and held it up as a bluff as she swept through the house, turning on lights and double-checking all the deadbolts.

Down in the garage, Bill had kept an old workbench, still cluttered with pliers, planers, hammers and screwdrivers. Among the many items, one in particular had always caught her eye, its blade partially hidden beneath a pack of sandpaper. She picked up the hatchet and bounced it in her hand. Like the pistol, the tool was small, lightweight, and if she had to use it, Vivienne felt confident she could handle the kick.

Back in the living room she covered Jeannie with an afghan, then curled up beside her with the hatchet beneath her pillow. The furnace kicked on. The house was bright.

Nothing to worry about … Nothing at all…

As Sheriff Andy Taylor told his son Opie about the time he got a black eye from a bully, Vivienne rolled over and tried to sleep.

***

Only vaguely aware of the noise which had disturbed her, Vivienne opened an eyelid. The breech of dawn lit the windows a tombstone gray. Something brushed her leg. It was Jeannie, who mumbled and rolled off the couch onto her feet.

A recurring whimper; that is what had wakened her. A high-pitched whine, like that of a feline, came from somewhere outside. Jeannie padded over to the front door wearing her footie pajamas. She pressed her ear against the white-painted wood.

"I think there's a cat outside," she said. She tried the knob and found it locked. Her little fingers went to the lock-switch and twisted it. Then her hand went to the deadbolt.

"Wait," Vivienne told her. She pulled the hatchet from beneath the pillow and slipped it inside her robe, beneath her arm. "Let me open it."

As she approached, the sound grew clearer—a mewling from right on the other side of the door. With an eye at the peephole, Vivienne scanned the front stoop, but saw nothing out of the ordinary. She slid the small wall-chain into the slot on the metal door plate, and unlocked the deadbolt. The opening spread about four inches before the chain caught.

A flash of motion. Vivienne gripped the hatchet. Something floated into view: a fish.

Vivienne fixed on the thing as her insides went cold and squirmy. The dead trout dangled from a fishing line that hung from a light in the awning above her front stoop. About a foot long, speckled and glistening, just like the ones in the cooler at the Food King, it rotated on the taut line, which gleamed perfectly straight in mid-air like the score of a razor in the very fabric of reality. The smell had lured the gray tomcat, who circled beneath the fish with his head tilted up, meowing eagerly.

"Shoo!" Vivienne said to the cat. "Get outta here, you little beggar!"

She wagged her foot at it, and the cat shot away a few feet, then turned around and waited out of reach.

"Is it that ol' stray again?" Jeannie asked from the foyer.

"Yes. Same old critter. Nothing to worry about." She turned to her granddaughter.

"I wasn't worried," Jeannie said.

"I know. Look, hon, why don't you go upstairs and put on your school clothes. You've got to catch the bus soon. I'll make you some Pop-Tarts."

"Yes, Pop-Tarts!" Jeannie exclaimed and hopped up the stairs to do as she was told.

In the kitchen, Vivienne poured herself a vodka eye-opener and grabbed a plastic bag to dispose of the fish.

Apparently Mizz Markessa had figured out how Vivienne had done her dirty deed. She must've seen the string. But if she wasn't taking that information to the police, Vivienne didn't see how it made one lick of difference.

***

At six twenty-five A.M., Vivienne squeezed her granddaughter tightly and waved goodbye as she boarded the school bus. As Jeannie claimed a seat and waved again through the window, Vivienne smiled and waved back, but the smile faded as the bus pulled away.

Never in all her years had anyone had the raw nerve to set foot on her property and leave a threat like that. A dead fish. Might as well be a horse's head. She supposed the woman might have meant to draw attention to the fishing line, but what mattered most was the message it sent. Mina wanted Vivienne to fear her next move. She wanted to make Vivienne's home feel unsafe. She wanted to creep into Vivienne's thoughts and plant seeds of paranoia, seeds that take root and spread like black ivy. Mina wanted to be seen hiding in every shadow and around each corner. Mina's message was meant to say: *"I'm coming for you, and you won't know when until it's too late."*

But Vivienne did not scare easily.

She lifted the plastic bag from her front stoop. She looped the fishing line around her fingers and lifted out the stinking fish before her face.

Mina's message, Vivienne realized, was actually more specific. *"I'm coming for you AND YOUR CHILD..."*

That familiar old heat surrounded Vivienne's collar, and blood pumped faster through her temples. *An eye for eye, and all that. That's what the bitch has in mind. But, mmm-mm-mmm ... No, ma'am, Mizz Markessa. You ain't touching my little Jeannie. Your heathen little daughter's already done enough of that, so you best cut your losses and drop this feud while you still got a head.*

She spun around, checked her own front stairs for any tripwires, then spiked her heels down the steps toward the road. She marched with her fists balled and swinging at her sides, the trout flapping at her thigh. Roadside, she waited for a station wagon to cruise by. It turned the corner, and Vivienne glanced around to find none of the other neighbors in sight. *Good.* She stepped up to the edge of the Markessa's property. Only the Tahoe remained in the driveway. The stuffed shirt had already gone to work. Mina and little Mushmouth must be inside, and maybe Kimmy too.

Vivienne saw no one through the Markessa's dark windows, but the blinds were angled partially open, much like she used for her own secret surveillance. And someone watched her. She felt eyes crawling over her like the tickling tips of spider legs, and knew she had Mina's attention.

Vivienne planted one hand on the hip of her jeans and with the other lifted up the trout like a weird trophy. "You don't scare me, Mizz Markessa!" she yelled at the house. "You and your fish can go straight to hell! You hear me? I'll leave *your* family alone if you leave *my* family alone! Got it?"

She hurled the fish at the neighbor's house. It flew farther than she'd expected and bounced with a *whap* off the red front door. It lay on the brick steps, on the third tread from the top, ogling up at the sky.

The house remained stubbornly quiet, but Vivienne held her ground in the standoff, staring down her unseen adversary with all the grit of a hardened cowboy. Mina was inside alright. And she was *watching*. Vivienne just knew it.

Her breath caught when the front door opened. It parted only a few inches, revealing a dark interior through a long black gash. From within the house something moved eye-level behind the door. A black pipe poked out of the opening. As it emerged from the house, Vivienne made out the horizontal barrel of a rifle, aimed right at her.

Oh shit.

With a gunpowder crack, an insect buzzed her ear. A pop from behind her preceded the crash of broken glass. Vivienne turned to see the shattered rear windshield of her parked Buick. A warm liquid tickled her neck on the left side, the same side where all sound now seemed muffled by cotton. The second rifle shot was quieter and missed by a wider margin, but it sure got her moving.

Crazy bitch is shooting! Right in front of God and everybody!

Vivienne wobbled as she fled across the street in heels. She made it to her lawn, and another gunshot barely missed her. A burst of dust exploded from the driveway that stretched across the grass. She scampered onto the brick walkway and reached the concrete front steps as the fourth shot struck her leg.

"Owwww dammit!" Vivienne shrieked and crashed onto her knees. At a glance, blood streaked her right thigh, but the tear looked superficial. In a rush of panic she scrambled up the front steps. Bouncing on her good left leg, she shouldered through the front door and slammed it behind her. The lock, bolt and chain all whammed home.

To avoid the front wall and any ensuing bullets, she hopped through the living room into the kitchen, where she crashed into a chair to catch her breath and check her injuries. Her knees bled and her leg throbbed, but she could manage the wounds. Her left ear burned, and her fingertip found the problem—the upper flap of cartilage had been nipped off by a bullet. That crazy witch had disfigured her.

The terror which had flooded over her now swelled and crashed with a fresh current of unbridled rage.

I'm ugly now. She made me ugly!

Vivienne stared at a blank spot on the wall, her stomach dropping into a deep pit as she mourned a face that would never look the same again. She'd need a new hairstyle to hide it. Water welled in her eyes.

The gunshots had paused. Maybe Mina had made her point. Or maybe Mina simply wanted her revenge up close and personal, saving the ammo for the whites of the eyes.

The hatchet.

Vivienne had left it on the living room coffee table.

She tried to crab-walk to get it, but her gashed thigh wouldn't cooperate. Keeping low to the ground and beyond the line of fire through the front windows, Vivienne frog-hopped across the carpet on her left leg, dragging her right behind her. She made it to the coffee table, snatched the hatchet and rolled to the front wall, just beneath a window sill. She scooted up against it and chanced a peek through the blinds.

Masked with a cold scowl of sheer malice, Mina Markessa had already crossed the street and was soldier-marching down Vivienne's walkway while raising the rifle eye level and aiming. Vivienne's jaw dropped before her whole body hit the floor.

The gunshot blasted splinters into the house from the door lock. Vivienne scrambled away from the wall and into the center of the room, scanning every direction for a place to hide.

With a bang, Mina tried to force the door in. With another ear-splitting blast, the wood jamb blew apart beside the deadbolt.

Just ten feet away, nothing separated that broken door from Vivienne but Bill's old green Lazy Boy recliner. The door shoved inward but caught on the interior chain. Vivienne saw Mina through the crack.

And Mina saw *her*.

With no time to think, Vivienne squeezed the hatchet with all her might and lunged into a loping sprint. Her right thigh screamed in torture but propelled her forward. She launched from the ball of her foot and found the seat of the recliner with her left shoe. Shoving off and gaining height, she soared through the room. Vivienne drew the hatchet up by her ear and aimed at Mina, who kicked the chained door open.

The rifle barrel flew up. The recliner tilted backward. A flash and a blast deafened Vivienne, but she kept her grip. The blade hurtled forward and struck with a *thwack!*

Mina dropped the gun and spilled backward through the doorway as Vivienne flew on top of her with a vicious shriek. Vivienne pulled the hatchet from Mina's cheek and chopped it back down again, cleaving open her lower jaw. The woman bucked, coughing up blood and teeth, but Vivienne had her pinned down. She wrenched out the hatchet and plunged it back down again. Then again. The final chop buried the blade deep into Mina's forehead with a wet crunch. Mina's arm spasmed at her side. The fingers curled and twisted wildy, then finally went still.

Gasping for air and weakened to the bone, Vivienne let go of the hatchet and pushed herself off Mina. She wiped her face with her sleeve and found the sharp sting of an open gash along her cheek.

Another graze from a bullet. Some might call her lucky, but she knew damned well what a mess she must look like.

She stood up shaking, every limb trembling like a weed in the wind.

A couple of neighbors had stopped along the roadside. One stepped out of his car and looked at her, and at the butchered body, but did not approach.

What most interested Vivienne was the bully, Kimmy Markessa, who stood watching from the street. She held Mina's bandaged baby and trembled just like Vivienne. The girl's face melted slowly into a quivering glower, and then she burst into squealing sobs of *"Mommy! Mommy! Oh no, noo, nooo! I want my mommy!"*

Vivienne wiped her hands on her blood-splattered blouse. It occurred to her this moment marked the first time she'd actually heard the rotten little girl say anything.

"Oh, *shut up!*" Vivienne snapped at her. The nerve of the little monster. "After all, *you* started it."

Then she limped inside her house and slammed the door.

Vivienne Reynolds needed a drink.

Silly Rabbits

The headlights shone a hundred feet ahead as the SUV rambled over a dirt road that ran alongside a barbed-wire fence. No other signs of civilization were in sight; only thick trees to one side, a rolling pasture on the other, and the bottomless black of night.

"Long drive," Harper said from the driver's seat.

"I trust you're not fucking with us," Freidman said to their navigator in the back seat.

Ned Hammond shook his head and wrapped his bulky coat tighter around his skinny frame. "Nobody's fucking with you," he said. "I'm not in the habit of taking two armed strangers out to the middle of the woods just to piss 'em off."

The Jeep Cherokee bounced over ridges and potholes.

"Who the hell lives in the dead center of nowhere?" Freidman muttered.

Ned gazed out the window. Darkness swallowed the entire countryside, although he knew that once they crested the next hill the cabin would come into view.

"The kind of person who lives out here is the kind of person who's trying to avoid people like you."

Neither of the bounty hunters replied. Freidman, a short man with a lizard-like face, lifted a flask and took a sip. He offered it to Harper, a barrel-chested man with a white goatee, who waved it away.

The vehicle took a downhill slope, and a dim orange light in the distance shone through the murk.

"That it up ahead?" Harper said.

"That's it," Ned said. "Kill the beams."

Harper turned off the headlights. As they descended toward the cabin, he slowed the Jeep to weave around the deep trenches carved into the road from runoff, the only light coming from a partial moon.

"Y'all need to get out," Ned said.

Harper hit the brakes. Freidman took another swig of his whiskey then closed it up in the glove box.

"This is close enough," Ned said. "He'll be watching. A man in his position tends to stay kinda jumpy. He sees you two riding with me, he's gonna suspect something's up."

"I thought you said he trusted you," Freidman said.

"I said I was friendly with him. But I ain't his friend. A man like that don't have friends, and he don't trust anybody."

"This better work, kid," Harper warned.

"Just stick to what we talked about. Y'all get out here, and I'll take the car down. I'll get him to come outside. You do what you're supposed to do, and everything'll be right as rain." Ned slipped his hand inside the pocket of his coat and squeezed the envelope full of cash, making sure it hadn't mysteriously vanished. "I get the other half when you get your man, right?"

Harper looked at Freidman. They nodded to one another.

"Keep up your end of the bargain and you'll get your money." Harper lifted a large black handgun from his lap. "If you pull any bullshit, I'll make damn sure one these silver bullets has your name on it."

Ned weighed his trust for the two men. It didn't weigh much. "Fair enough."

Harper shifted into park. They exited the cab and collected their gear from the back before Ned climbed behind the steering wheel.

"It shouldn't take long. Just stay with the plan and remember—we have a deal." Ned shut the door and weaved the SUV down the hill toward the lone cabin.

***

James Harper slipped five silver-tipped cartridges into a .44 revolver and holstered it on his right hip. On his left hung a nine-millimeter loaded with a full clip of hollow points. He lifted a red gas can off the ground, and then pushed a machete through a sheath on his belt. Death by silver, fire, or full decapitation. Harper firmly believed in redundant methods of execution—just in case.

He looked at Freidman and nodded his head at the cabin. "Let's go. You take right, I'll flank left. Stay out of sight. We wrap around the corners of the house, take them from behind as they exit the front. I'll make the first move. You cover me. Don't let him get to the Jeep."

Freidman nodded. "Why the arsenal? You don't really believe what they say about this guy?"

"I'm not taking any chances." Harper looked into the sky at a crescent moon made hazy by clouds.

"But, seriously. You don't actually think it takes a silver bullet to kill this guy? It's all so stupid. You don't really believe all this bullshit?"

"I believe in money," Harper said with gravel in his voice. "I believe in getting the job done. Mr. White believes that this man is a lycanthrope, and he's willing to pay a lot of money for us to deliver the package. I expect to collect a handsome fee for my services, and I will use any means necessary to protect myself while doing the job. That's all that matters."

"But—"

"No buts." Harper turned away. "Let's get to work." He marched toward the left of the house.

Freidman slinked away in the other direction.

The deep night and a thin moon concealed their approach. The front porch of the cabin flickered from a lamp hanging on a nail. Harper heard no hum of a generator, and the dancing light indicated the open flame of oil or a candle. The place likely had no electricity.

Although a big man, Harper was fit and powerful, and moved with agile grace while staying low to the ground as he neared the wall of the house.

Remain invisible; remain silent, he coached himself.

Aside from the whisper of wind through the nearby pines, the night remained remarkably quiet; nothing like the noisy city Harper called home. The quiet helped him focus, to keep an edge. He pressed his ear close to the old clapboard wood siding to hear the muffled voices within the cabin. He could not make out the words, but the exchange sounded casual and relaxed. The boy and the man were having a conversation, a fairly unexciting one. That was good.

A rattle and scrape from around the corner told Harper the men were exiting through the front door and stepping onto the porch. Clinging to the shadows, he inched forward with his revolver raised and his shoulder to the wall. He peered around the edge of the house and saw the kid in his puffy coat and a taller man in red-and-black flannel. They each held bottles of beer and stepped off the porch onto the grass.

Harper made his move.

"Stay where you are, both of you!" he commanded.

Ned and the other man froze. Harper closed in fast, arcing around them with the gun leveled, circling to face them. When he met their eyes he cocked the hammer, a move he always saved until the mark was watching because he liked its dramatic effect.

"Who are you?" said the man in the flannel. The lantern behind him revealed little more than his silhouette: tall, slim and muscular, with full black hair and a shade of stubble at the edges of his face.

"Who I am doesn't matter," Harper said as he clicked on a bright flashlight which caused the man to squint and wince. "What matters is that you fit the description of one George Davis Caufield, and that makes you a wanted man. I'm here to bring you in."

In the dim light behind them, Freidman emerged from the far side of the house with his gun drawn, creeping forward. "Back up, kid," he said to Ned, "we gonna take him into custody."

"Ned?" asked the man in flannel. "Do you know these men?"

Ned looked at everyone, back and forth, then shrugged and backed away. "Me? Hey, no, I don't know. Look, I was just doing what I gotta do. I mean, you know how it is, George."

"George Caufield," Harper said. "I will keep this gun aimed at your heart while my associate behind you places cuffs around your wrists. We will escort you to the vehicle where your ankles will be bound as well. If you give us any problem whatsoever, I will pull the trigger on this .44 and will continue to fire it until I'm out of ammunition. Do you understand what I am telling you?"

Caufield looked around. His chest heaved, and he grunted under his breath.

"*Do you understand?*" Harper persisted.

The man seethed. "Yes."

"You guys are going to pay up, right?" Ned said.

"Shut the fuck up, kid." Harper growled.

"But you owe me. We had a deal."

A spike of irritation shot through Harper's temple. He gave Freidman a razor-edged glance and a quick nod. Freidman pivoted his aim, and with a night-cracking *POW!* shot Ned in the back.

Ned gasped and pitched forward. With lightning speed Harper swiveled and fired a bullet at Ned's ribs. The kid dropped to the ground.

Instantly, Harper's aim returned to Caufield. "We are serious men, and this is serious business. Our employer prefers that you be delivered alive, but I have a very short temper. You will do as you're instructed, or I will inflict pain upon you unlike anything you've ever experienced. And if necessary I will end your life completely. Nobody fucks with me. Remember that."

Caufield slowly nodded.

"Freidman, move in."

Freidman jangled the restraints out of his pocket and met no resistance as he cuffed the taller man and shoved him toward the SUV.

Harper opened the door, spun Caufield around and backed him into the vehicle with the gun in his face. He held him there while Freidman strapped layers of duct tape around the man's ankles. Caufield had a gaunt face with sunken eyes and appeared to be drunk. He didn't look like much to Harper, not like the usual slippery criminal masterminds he encountered on big-money jobs like this one.

With their captive adequately immobilized, Harper closed the door to the back seat. Freidman went to where Ned lay and retrieved the envelope of cash from his pocket, while Harper climbed into the Jeep and started the engine.

The plan was moving along smoothly. With Freidman at his side Harper steered onto the dusty trail that led to the highway and out of this hayseed backcountry.

Freidman sat side-saddle and held the gun on Caufield, who lay sprawled across the rear bench seat.

"You don't look too hairy to me," Freidman said to the man in back. Harper could hear the smirk in his voice. "Not exactly scary, either."

Caufield said nothing and only breathed heavily.

Freidman continued, "No, I don't think you look much like a monster at all. I think it's all bullshit."

The Jeep angled uphill, shaking and swaying as Harper dodged the pits and ditches of the road. Freidman grabbed the seat's headrest to steady himself. He leaned over and stared at Caufield.

"What I don't understand," Freidman said, "is why other people believe this bullshit. And believe it to the point where they're willing to pay so much damn cash for us to deliver you with a big, red bow. You mind telling me how the hell something like that happens to a guy like you?"

Harper heard a rustling behind him and saw the man sit up in the rearview mirror.

Caufield stuck out his bottom jaw and blew the stringy, black bangs out of his face. "What exactly have you heard about me?"

Freidman spread a wide smile that shone through the darkness. "Don't you know? You're supposed to be a werewolf! A goddamn *wolfman!*" Freidman snickered as he said this, then puckered his lips and howled, *"Arrrooooooooo!"* which he punctuated with a peal of laughter.

While fighting the bumpy road, Harper kept an eye on the captive in the mirror. The shadowy figure over his shoulder did not respond or even move for a very long time.

"A werewolf?" the man finally said.

"Yeah," Freidman said. "How the hell you think we found you? Your dumbass friend back there sold you out on some sort of werewolf-hunter website. The type of place where geeks and crazies trade lies and hoaxes. But every once in a while, crazy rich bastards will hang out there, too. They buy into the tall tales of some hillbilly, and pay us to follow up. Then, *ta-da! …* We show up at your doorstep."

"I'm not a werewolf."

"Hmm. Well, I guess it wouldn't matter much to me if you were or not, less you got all fanged-out on me," Freidman said. "I mean, ain't a full moon out tonight, so I guess we're safe. Right? I just don't understand how these stories get started, or go as far as they do. That's the big mystery to me: not whether monsters exist, but how human beings can be so damn stupid."

Caufield nodded in agreement, slow and knowing like a gesture of confidence, and this put Harper on guard.

"You're right about that," their captive said. "Humans can be very stupid."

"It is a burden the rest of us have to bear," Freidman said.

"Take you two, for instance," Caufield said. "I was just minding my own business, leading a peaceful, solitary existence. And you two drive out to the middle of the woods to seek your fortune at my expense."

"We're bounty hunters," Freidman said. "That's the name of the game."

"But it's not a game," the man said. "You've made a hell of a mistake. You see, you're not the hunters in this scenario. You are the hunted. Now you're going to die out here. In the middle of nowhere, where no one will ever find you."

"Is that right, motherfucker?" Freidman's voice tightened like a screw. "How you figure that? Seein' as I've got a Glock pointed at your fucking face."

Harper's heart thumped in his chest. Freidman should shut up and stop antagonizing the situation, but his partner was right. They had the upper hand. So why did the nerves tingle in Harper's ear? Why were his palms sweating? It was because of the confidence in the stranger's voice. Harper hated the bound man's cocksure certainty.

"Your gun won't help you," Caufield said. "You won't even make it back to the main road. I'm going to tear you to pieces out here in the woods."

Freidman's jaw dropped with dumbfounded astonishment. He looked at Harper. "You hear what this sonofabitch just said?"

With a sudden bang, Freidman's face wrenched with a piercing scream.

Harper slammed the brake. The Jeep slid and tilted, jarring to a stop as a tire found a trench.

Freidman's head bounced off the windshield and left a crack. A gurgling moan spilled from his throat as a gnarled claw of long, bony talons burst out of his buttoned shirt. The dripping appendage had hook-like nails that sunk back into Freidman's gut and groped inside. George Caufield roared inhumanly from behind, and then jerked Freidman back into the seat.

Harper, in blind terror, plastered himself against the door of the Jeep. He screamed as the vehicle quaked and rumbled.

Caufield's shirt stretched and split apart from his swelling girth as he snarled and groped at Freidman. In a wild fury Caufield tried to pull him through the new cavity in the backrest—but the body was too big to fit. Freidman's torso folded in half at the waist as Caufield ripped his spine through the hole, but it snagged at his head. With a brutal yank, the head finally pulled through the seat atop the bloody spine like soap on a rope. The gored corpse collapsed into a pile and bled in the front seat.

The creature grew and changed shape in the back of the Jeep, morphing from man to huge black beast, something with pronged horns and hot, acrid breath. Its teeth snapped Freidman's skull in half with a single bite.

A blithering mess, Harper slapped for the door handle. *Run, oh God! Just run! Oh God! Where's the handle!* He looked for the lever and saw the guns on his belt. The silver bullets!

He drew the revolver and fired into the creature five times, until the chamber clicked empty.

Now deaf with his ears ringing, Harper stared in horror as the thing grew and grew, never even flinching from the bullets that blazed through its flesh. The hulking form pressed against the roof of the car and bowed the metal. With a screech and a pop, the roof peeled away, and the thing shot up into the night and disappeared.

Wind stirred inside the vehicle, swirling around Harper, who had his hand on his heart to check his pulse rate. His breathing came quick and shallow. He scoured the sky. Then he rose up and scanned the countryside. Cloaked by the night, the thing that had been George Caufield could be anywhere, just out of sight, eyeballing its next course while sharpening its claws.

Get ahold of yourself. Calm down. Concentrate. Consider your options.

The silver bullets hadn't worked. Harper had the gas can in the back, but no way to deploy it now that his captive had broken free of the restraints. He had the machete, but dreaded getting close enough to the monster to use it.

And that's what this thing was … a *monster*. What else could you call it? A *monster* had killed Freidman.

The car shook as a heavy thud struck the earth just beyond reach of the headlights, which shined obliquely across the dirt path. Something big moved in the darkness ahead.

With the engine still idling, Harper straightened in his seat, dropped into first gear and floored it. The motor revved, and the wheels hummed, but the SUV went nowhere. The tires caught no traction. Harper rocked and thrust in his seat, trying to tilt the car, to weigh it down on the road so the tread would bite. Again, he hit the gas, but the Jeep stayed put.

The creature roared and stepped into the yellow light. The size of ten men, the huge black thing looked more beast than human, and more bat than wolf. Gigantic, membranous wings spread from its back in a bus-length span. It stalked forward in a hungry prowl on scythe-like talons that rattled with every step. Puffs of vapor wafted from its snout, and two deep-set eyes flickered like bright red flame.

Having regained composure, Harper knew one thing damn well: This creature had his number. Hard to deny that. Yet, as he sat in the now-convertible car like an oyster on a half shell, Harper began to fume. So what if he'd met his match. So fucking *what*. That didn't matter. What mattered was that this creature had come face to face with *James mother-fucking Harper,* one man who refused to go down without a fight.

He grabbed Freidman's flask from the glove box, pulled off the cap and sucked down a huge shot of throat-burning whiskey. Then he untwisted his partner's fingers from the nine-millimeter dangling from his hand. He opened the Jeep door, drew his own backup sidearm, and wrapped his fingers around both triggers.

As Harper stepped into the light of the headlamps, the creature lowered its horned head and growled deeply, a cavernous sound that smoldered and echoed across the emptiness. Two slender serpentine tails emerged from behind it, writhing like skeletal whips. Each tail brandished a sharp, spiny tip. The tails snaked upward, then arched and hovered above.

Harper tightened his grip, raised both barrels and aimed. "George Davis Caufield," he said to the thing. "I fucking warned you."

In hot, white flashes, the guns blasted through the night, exploding the quiet and calm. With clenched-teeth ferocity Harper squeezed harder and faster as he marched ahead. The bullets plunged into the thing. It shuddered and hissed, and even backed away. Anger fueled Harper with high-octane rage as he gained ground, his blood pumping with lava-like adrenaline.

The hail of ammunition finally ran dry as the incendiary blasts softened to a *click-click-click*. The smell of cordite burned Harper's nostrils.

The demonic thing quivered in a mound.

After a moment it peered up.

Harper stared at its wounds. They leaked a viscous fluid. He'd wounded the thing. That meant he could kill it. Harper drew the machete. He lowered his shoulder and lunged forward with charging speed.

One of those spindly tails darted forth and speared him in the chest. It was like he hit an invisible wall. The sting went from a searing pinprick in his sternum to a full-chest inferno. The blade fell from his hand. Harper shook from head to toe as the creature's long, gnarled appendage, rigid and spine-like, pumped something into him which extinguished the initial wave of blazing pain with a narcotic numbness. The opiate effect spread through his body and warmed his brain, making the world fuzzy, filling him with a comfortable coziness that invited rest and relaxation and a wholly untroubled slumber.

***

Harper had no way of knowing how many hours—or days— he'd been unconscious when he opened his eyes.

What happened? Where am I? Another planet?

The world appeared alien and unworkable, until Harper realized that he hung upside down from the top of a very tall tree, at a dizzying height.

He twisted and wiggled but found himself cocooned in some sort of sticky, plaster-like material which squeezed his legs together and pressed his arms to his sides. Only his head remained uncovered, and it throbbed with the pressure of collected blood. He parted his lips to scream but no sound escaped. As the sun rose in the distance and sent faint orange rays across the hilly countryside, he saw only an expansive forest surrounding him and a distant fence-lined pasture.

Sure screwed the pooch on this one, Harper thought as he breathed deeply, and a fresh dose of mind-numbing relief surged through him. Despite his predicament, at least he didn't feel so bad. The view was nice. And the place was peaceful. Quiet.

Things could always be worse.

***

Ned awoke to a thump against his breast. He batted his eyes open to the cloudy sky of a breaking dawn. He lay in the same patch of grass where he'd fallen the previous night, now cold and wet with dew. A small paper sack lay crumpled on his chest. He took it in hand and could tell by the flex and heft it was full of cash.

"Got your money back," said a familiar voice. "Plus, a lot more."

Ned gave a long, aching sigh. Then he smiled as the man stepped into view. "That's what I like to hear," Ned said and reached up with his hand. George Caufield took it and helped him to his feet.

Ned's informational website and message-board, www.WerewolvesAreReal.org, attracted mainly horror fans, history buffs, conspiracy theorists and genuine crazies. But it occasionally lured the very serious inquiry, posed by very wealthy individuals who sought things that nobody else had.

With a sore chest, Ned unsnapped his heavy coat and unstrapped the Kevlar jacket that had awaited him inside George's cabin. He figured himself a pretty good judge of character since the two bounty hunters behaved exactly like he had them pegged;

Freidman was the sort that'd shoot you in the back, while Harper would look you dead in the eye and do it. He peeked inside the paper sack and whistled. "This job turned out real nice. How things go on your end?"

George wore a clean white undershirt, a jean jacket, and looked no worse or worn than when Ned had last seen him. "Right as rain. I reckon I ate my fill," he said and gazed into the forest. "Got the leftovers curing in a tree for later in the week."

A shudder coursed through Ned and turned his stomach. He and George were friendly, but they weren't friends.

"Good, that's good," Ned said. "I already got a lead on the next one. Some bigwig over in England comin' stateside in a couple weeks. Says he wants to hunt the kind of game he can't find over there."

George shook his head. "Werewolves..."

"Yep, *werewolves*." Ned figured a sucker was born every minute, and he was ready and eager to make their acquaintance. "Silly rabbits. Everybody knows werewolves ain't real." He gave his associate a wink and a chuckle.

The sun broke over the horizon and gleamed like fire in George Caufield's eyes. "That's right," he said. "Silly rabbits."

Of All the Nights

Wanda Hanover's mobile phone vibrated on the coffee table.

"Don't answer it." A black-gloved thumb pulled back the hammer on the revolver pointed at her chest.

Wanda did as she was told. She put her hands in her lap, scooted back on the sofa and watched the phone buzz. The name *Irene* glowed on its screen. She'd been expecting a call from Irene Henderson up the road.

"Be cool and be quiet," the man told her. "I got no reason to hurt you, unless you give me one."

He wore chocolate-colored alligator boots. He had faded black jeans and a big brass belt-buckle that read, *Save a Tree, Eat a Beaver.* Wanda tried not to look at his face. She'd bolted the front door of the house earlier in the evening; they must have picked the lock of another or somehow used a window to break in.

"Please," she said, as a lump swelled in her throat. "Take whatever you want. I'll cooperate. Just don't hurt us. That's all I ask."

The gun twitched. "Who's 'us'?"

"Hey Mom, they got the chickens from the Henderson place! They've made it over here to our street!" The young voice, loud and excited, shouted from the doorway behind her. Wanda's heart sank. With a trample of footsteps, her twelve-year-old son clambered upstairs from the basement. He threw open the door. "They're here, Mom! They're really he—"

Bryan went quiet as the second man straightened his arm to aim a gun at him. The second man was taller, more muscular and darker than the first, based on the skin tones beneath the haze of their pantyhose masks.

"What's going on, Mom?"

"What's it look like?" the second man said. "Walk your ass—slowly—over to the couch and sit next to your mother. Is anybody else in the house?"

Wanda shook her head. "No. My husband is—"

"—dead," the first man said. "Yeah, we know."

That they knew of her husband's passing told her the reason these men had invaded her home. Edward Hanover had amassed a great deal of money once upon a time. For two decades the Hanover family owned and operated the coal mine at the foot of the mountain. Faced with crushing regulations, the coal business had gone belly-up over the last several years, and the money dried up with it. This was done by governmental design on the altar of "greener living," even though it meant the lives of many miners went gray in the aftermath. Edward had tried everything to avoid layoffs. Despite his best efforts, the mine closed. When the workers searched for someone to blame, they pointed to the man at the top, at least the one they could see. The weight of it all proved too much for his heart to take.

These two men were likely some of those angry people, driven by desperation, greed and a misplaced sense of revenge. And they'd chosen the most dangerous night of all for a caper on Blackstone Mountain.

"Where's the safe?" the first man asked her.

"We don't have a safe," Bryan said. "Y'all are trying to rob us? Are you crazy? Don't you know what tonight is?"

"Stop talking, Bryan," Wanda said.

"Listen to your mother," the first man said.

"But Mom, Todd sent me a text! The Henderson's chickens are gone!"

With a sharp crack, the second man's gun smashed across Bryan's face, knocking him back against the couch. Wanda seized up as if she'd been the one struck. She swept over and wrapped an arm around him. He teared up as blood ran from a gash in his peach-fuzzy cheek.

The second man leaned over Bryan and pointed at the butt of his gun. "Open your mouth again and I'll close it permanently."

"Please!" Wanda pleaded, trying not to cry. "I told you we'd cooperate. Just don't hurt us."

"What's with all the chickens, anyway?" the first man asked. "I hate to break it to you, but your chickens are gone too. They wouldn't shut the fuck up when we were making our entrance." He made a slicing gesture across his neck.

Bryan's mouth fell open. The two chickens had been placed in the coop outside to serve a very important purpose. "Oh no…"

Again, the second man drew his gun back, but Wanda threw herself onto Bryan, holding up her hands and wincing in anticipation of the blow.

It didn't come.

"I told you to shut up!" he said, lowering the pistol. "Anyway, screw the chickens. Where's the cash?"

The phone on the coffee table chimed with an incoming text from Irene. From the sofa Wanda could see the screen, which read: *It's happening.*

"Yeah, where's the valuables?" the first man said. "Make us rich quick, and we'll get outta your hair."

To be quick was crucial. If these men did not leave the house soon, no one here would see another sunrise.

The larger man pulled a roll of duct tape from his jacket and ripped off a long strip. "Give me your hands," he told Bryan, then bound the boy's wrists and ankles.

"We do have a safe," Wanda said. "It's in the wall of our bedroom closet. I'll take you to it. But first—"

"No buts. Let's go," the first man said.

"Did you come through a door or a window?" she persisted.

"The safe. Now."

"I just want to make sure it's closed. The door or window. Did you close it behind you?"

"Dammit, your back door is closed, okay?" he griped. "What are you, fuckin' OCD? The safe. *Now!*"

"I'll be right back," Wanda told Bryan, whose face had paled with fear.

She stood up and led them toward the hallway, praying the man was telling the truth about the back door. All entrances to the house had to remain closed—those were the rules, and she dared not break them.

She took them both to the last room on the right and opened the door. The sight of the bed made her queasy.

They pushed past her and headed straight to the closet. The first one gestured at it with his gun. "In here?"

She nodded.

"Open it."

Wanda slipped past them and into the walk-in closet. She flipped a switch. The room brightened. Her clothes hung on the left along with racks of shoes and a chest of drawers. Edward's wardrobe occupied the opposite wall. Wanda slipped both hands between two of his suits and spread her arms. The clothes slid apart along the closet rod to reveal a wall-mounted safe.

"Get busy with the digits," the first man said.

She spun the combination dial a few full rotations to the left, then landed the indicator at 33.

"This all the loot you got around here?" the bigger man asked her.

With three turns to the right, the dial stopped at 47.

"We got the safe, man," the first one said to him. "If she's got anything else hidden, she ain't gonna say so."

Two turns to the left, and Wanda rested the indicator on the final number, 62. She tugged on the door. It didn't budge.

"What gives?" the first man said.

"I must have messed up the combination," Wanda said.

The second man's gun smacked against her head, and stars exploded in her vision. She pitched forward, but braced herself against the safe. "That jog your memory, bitch?"

"Take it easy, she's a woman," the first one said.

"I'm sorry," Wanda muttered, "I'll try again." She shut her eyes and cleared her head of dizziness. The point of impact on her scalp throbbed with heat, and a warm trickle inched down between the hairs on the back of her neck.

She spun the dial furiously and landed on 33.

"Mom, I hear something outside!" Bryan called from the other end of the house.

With three turns to the right, Wanda stopped the dial at 74.

"Maybe you should go check that out," the first man said to his partner, jerking his head in the direction of Bryan's voice.

"Shit." The big one walked out of the room.

Two turns to the left finished the combination at 62. Wanda tugged on the knob, and the safe's door floated open. Stacked inside were three envelopes full of cash and a wooden box of jewelry. The first man shoved her aside and gathered the goods, including the diamond engagement ring given to her by the only man she'd ever loved.

"You got it?" the second man asked as he reappeared in the bedroom doorway.

"I got it. What was the noise?"

"I didn't hear nothing. Kid's full of shit. Says it's dangerous to leave."

"What? Whatever," the first man said. "Let's roll."

Wanda followed them back to the living room where Bryan was bound. As they walked for the front door, Bryan said, "Wait, y'all can't leave. Mom, tell 'em."

The men hesitated. They exchanged a glance.

Wanda looked at her shoes and refused to answer. And as she did, shame crept out of the floor and filled her.

"Mom, you let 'em leave and it's murder! Even if they're robbers, they don't deserve that!"

She focused on her slippers—red sheepskin moccasins with fleece lining to keep her feet warm. They'd been a gift from Edward. Now that he was gone, Bryan was all she had left.

"The fuck is this kid talkin' about?" the second man said.

"Forget him. Like you said, he's full of shit."

"Something's out there!" Bryan said. "Tonight's Blackstone Passover! You go outside and you're good as dead!"

"The what?" the second man asked.

"Local fairy tales. I've heard it before," the first one answered. "A bunch of crap. Let's go."

Blackstone Mountain—or something *inside* the mountain— willingly offered its vast natural resources to the people who lived here, but it always expected something in return. And once a year, on Blackstone Passover, it was time for the people of the mountain to keep up their end of the bargain.

"It's *true*! Tell 'em, Mom!"

Everyone stared at her. She met their eyes, and then looked away from them all. She turned her back on her son, and in doing so, showed him the runner of blood that trailed down her neck and stiffened the fabric on the collar of her blouse.

"They killed the chickens, Bryan," she said. "They killed the chickens..." A grave coldness gripped her, an empty feeling she feared might never leave her after tonight. Her son's heart was in the right place by trying to warn them, but she knew the cost of such selflessness. The mountain demanded a sacrifice. "Just let them go."

Whether due to his mother's words or the sight of the blood, Bryan said nothing else.

"Let's get the hell out of here," the first man said. He pressed the unlock button on the front door. His gloved fingers clutched the knob. Wanda held her breath. He opened the door with a slight squeak to the exterior darkness. The wind howled, and Wanda braced for a flood of nightmares to crash into her home and consume them all.

But the man walked outside without incident. His partner followed, and they both stole away into the night.

The glow of the living room lamps lit the small wire coop outside at the foot of the stoop. The two chickens lay in white lumps, unmoving.

Wanda slammed the door. She threw the deadbolt and pressed the electronic lock button on the knob. With a deep sigh of relief, she spun and pressed her back to the slab and slid halfway down to the floor. The sight of Bryan bound with duct tape got her moving again.

She rushed over and pulled at the tape. Getting nowhere, she ran to the kitchen and returned with a steak knife.

"What's gonna happen to them?" Bryan asked as she cut through his restraints.

A scream from outside made her freeze. Bryan's eyes widened. The scream rose up and stretched out, carrying a shrill note of terror that stippled Wanda's skin with gooseflesh.

Three more strokes of the blade freed his hands.

"Mommm…" Bryan's voice wavered. He made a whimpering sound and pressed his head against her shoulder. She dropped the knife and threaded her fingers into his hair as she hugged him.

Another voice sounded from the front yard. Frantic cursing grew louder and louder as it got closer to the house. After a patter of footsteps, the fiberglass front door shook with impact and then thundered with the pounding of fists.

"Let me in, lady! Holy shit, you gotta let me back in!" It sounded like the second man, but a voice so high-pitched with panic it was hard to tell.

Bryan squeezed his mother tighter.

"Just tune it out," she cooed into his ear. "Just tune it out."

"There's something out here … *It's gonna kill me out here!* … *HELP ME, LADY!*" the man's voice pealed away into an incoherent squeal as something heavier slammed into the door where he stood. The front wall shook, and everything outside banged and clattered.

Wanda held Bryan like she had when he was a baby, pressing her cheek to his own.

The man's gagging and cursing dwindled to grunts and finally went quiet. The rest of the night went silent as well. All was still.

Bryan asked, "Is it over?"

Wanda sighed. "It's over."

He sniffed and wiped his eyes. "I can't believe that we … that we just let it happen."

She fixed on the front door, finding a new appreciation for its strength and sturdiness as she gathered her thoughts. She then faced her son. "No, honey. You can't think that way. There was nothing we could do. If the mountain doesn't get an offering, the things it sends to collect will come inside and take whatever they want. It's always been that way. But it's over now. And we have to remember what's important. And what is important is that we still have each other." She looked deep into his eyes. "Do you understand?"

Bryan rubbed his nose and averted his gaze. He hung his head and shook it sadly as he walked away. He paused in the doorway at the top of the staircase as if to say something.

Please say something, she thought.

But he quietly descended the steps to his room.

Wanda couldn't sleep.

Alone, she watched the sun come up.

Burt's Top Secret Spice Mix

Cheeseburger-No-Pickles walked into the sandwich shop wearing his blue workshirt from the Auto Depot. Burt greeted him with a wave and said, "Doing all right today?"

"Doing fine, Burt. You?"

"Fine as French wine, my friend. Want the usual?"

"You bet."

Burt, scooped a meat patty off the griddle and flipped it onto a bun along with a slice of cheese. He added lettuce, onions, a squirt of mustard, and topped it off with a hosing of Burt's Special Sauce—which was a drastically different formulation than Burt's Top Secret Spice Mix—and presented it to the customer.

"One cheeseburger, no pickles, and a bottle of root beer. That'll be five-fifty."

Cheeseburger-No-Pickles gave Burt exact change and slipped an extra dollar into the tip jar beside the cash register.

"Thank you, sir," Burt said.

"No, thank *you*." The man took his lunch and left.

The prep area of the narrow shop lined the left-hand wall, allowing room for only a few stools along the counter that ran up the middle. Most folks took their food to go.

The glass door opened and two more customers approached the counter. The first was Hotdog-No-Relish, which the little gray-haired lady always specified, even though Burt didn't offer relish as a standard condiment.

Behind Hotdog-No-Relish stood That Fat Bastard Larry Azalea, which struck Burt as incredibly odd because Larry had supposedly died yesterday. Burt had seen the report on the evening news. And Larry had died after ingesting a heavy dose of Burt's Top Secret Spice Mix.

A chill prickled Burt's skin. He focused his attention on the lady, although he felt the man's eyes chisel away at him. "Doing well, ma'am?"

She smiled, nodded and dug into her purse for money. Burt doctored up her hotdog and slid her the tray, including the sweet tea with lemon she always drank with lunch.

"Have a nice day, Mr. Burt," she said after paying. Her usual tip, a quarter, clinked into the bottom of the jar.

"You too, sweetheart," he said as she left. "See you soon."

Burt didn't want to look, but had no choice. He turned to the next customer, who stood with his arms crossed on the other side of the plexiglass partition which separated the cooktop from the dining area. The man had a huge gut and held a toothpick between his teeth. He stared coldly at Burt.

"Can I help you?" Burt asked.

Larry had black hair slicked to his scalp, a black button-up shirt and dark slacks. His head cocked to one side as if he expected Burt to say something else. But Burt kept quiet.

"Don't you know my order?" Larry asked.

The two were alone. Burt's young employee, Grady, had gone to the grocery store to fetch more buns, since their usual supplier had shorted the weekly order.

Burt held Larry's gaze with his best poker face, acting as though nothing were out of the ordinary, and said, "French fries with ranch sauce, and a foot-long chili-cheese-slaw-dog."

Larry looked out the window toward the cars passing down Grayson Drive, and then turned back to Burt. "Is that the name you have for me?"

Burt shook his head. "No." He was terrible with names but a whiz at remembering orders. Assignment of a nickname based on a food order, however, was an honor he privately bestowed on regular patrons, and not on lowlifes like the man in present company. How Larry knew about the name game puzzled him.

"You make that order," Larry said. "But leave out the special ingredient you added yesterday. The one that killed me."

Burt threw a glance around the shop to make sure nobody had heard him. The place was empty. And cold. Much colder than usual. Had Grady monkeyed with the thermostat?

"Coming right up." Burt went to work on the dish. He rolled the charred frank across the griddle to sear the casing. He plunked it into a split bun and piled on the spicy chili, shredded cheddar, special sauce and creamy coleslaw. A thick layer of ranch dressing topped off Larry's basket of fries, and Burt filled a Mega Gulp beverage container with a quart of Dr. Pepper. Where the partition ended, he slid the order across the counter to Larry. "Hope you enjoy it."

"Go fuck yourself," Larry said with murder in his eyes.

Burt again looked around. This dreamlike exchange made him doubt himself, his health and his mind. Larry could not possibly be here, unless the Channel 6 News had gotten the story wrong. Or ... maybe Burt was the wrong one. Had he really seen last night's report or imagined it? At sixty-eight, he knew his spry years were behind him, but he'd never had a problem with his gray matter. Not yet.

He knew one thing with perfect clarity. Yesterday he'd slipped his Top Secret Spice Mix—ground monkshood, enough to kill a cow, and supposedly untraceable—on top of Larry's hotdog before scooping the chili over it. Yet, Larry had returned today for another foot-long, which could only mean he survived.

Larry grabbed his tray and stepped over to his usual stool at the end of the counter. He did not pay for his food. Larry never paid. That's one of the reasons Burt had poisoned him.

***

Yesterday, Larry Azalea left Burt's Super Sandwich Shop with a plastic bib tucked into his collar. He ran a comb through his hair, wiped sauce from his chin, and snatched off the bib which fell as litter to the parking lot. The afternoon was hot and getting hotter. He opened the door to his Cadillac. With the car cranked, the air conditioner blew cold wind across his face, refreshing him. Calming him, because he'd been feeling short of breath.

The Cadillac rolled smoothly onto Grayson Drive heading for Main Street. Larry's lunch of ranch fries and a chili-cheese-slaw-dog roiled inside his stomach. Wednesday was delivery day for the local merchants, and the extra trucks congested traffic and slowed his drive home. Despite having the AC at full blast, a fuzzy blanket of heat clung to his skin. It would feel good to lie down and get off his feet.

A red street light brought the car to a stop. His belly gurgled, and a pocket of gas climbed through him and belched out his mouth. It stunk like chili. The temperature of the car continued to rise. Maybe some sort of fire *inside* him. He lived with acid indigestion every day of his life, but something deep in his gut fizzed and sizzled with unusual strength.

Larry's breathing became quick and shallow. He tried to suck in great gulps of air, but an invisible restriction clutched his lungs, and held them small and empty. A sudden urge to pee gripped him. The car constricted around him.

Why won't the red light turn green? Is there no oxygen in this damned thing?

He slapped at the switch on the door. The electric windows inched downward. He stuck out his face and gasped for fresh air, but found the world outside just as empty.

"What the hell?!" he gagged with no voice. Still a red light. He had to get out of here. Had to get help.

His foot punched the gas pedal. The Caddy bucked forward. It rolled into the intersection. A horn blared from his right. A shadow closed in.

The impact sent the world spinning. Glass sliced the flesh of his face. White flashes of light. Hard angles bit and bashed him as he tumbled in a crunching metal cage. That heat never left. The air never came, but the flames did. Once the car stopped moving, his face lay mashed against a spider-webbed window, and his neck kinked beneath his weight. Fire surrounded him. Voices somewhere nearby cried for help. But he saw there would be no time. He could not move his limbs. He could not draw a breath, and his skull threatened to pop. The fire began eating the shoes and flesh of his feet, the sensation more akin to intense cold than heat—at least at first.

"Help me..." Larry closed his eyes and begged any higher power listening to please let him asphyxiate before the flames claimed any more.

***

"Man, slow day, huh?"

Grady's voice snapped Burt out of a daze. The kid emerged from the back wearing his uniform baseball hat and bearing two full bread trays. He racked them on the shelves, took a few packs out, and commenced tearing open the plastic and sorting the buns into bins on the prep counter. "Anybody been in since I've been gone?" he asked Burt.

Larry sat on the opposite side of the clear plexi from where Grady stacked the buns, maybe three feet away and in plain view.

"You don't see any customers?" Burt asked him.

Grady lifted up and swiveled his head around, searching the room, looking right through Larry yet showing no notice. "No. You do?" He arched his brow.

Burt had to think fast. "Out back, I mean. You didn't see anyone headed this way? None of our regulars?" A reasonable cover-up, he thought; the rear of the store opened into a parking lot. Burt was acutely aware of Larry smirking at him throughout this exchange but he refused to make eye contact.

"Nada," Grady said.

Egg-Sandwich-with-Mustard burst through the door with his arms open. "Burt, my man! How's it goin'? Is this a beautiful day, or is this a beautiful day?"

"Finally," Grady mumbled.

Egg-Sandwich-with-Mustard was a rarity: a man with two names. Over the years Burt had learned that Ronnie Johnson not only liked his eggs over-easy, but also ran a dry cleaners in the same plaza as the sandwich store. And Ronnie had to endure the same extortionist assholes that Burt had to put up with, which gave the two a common bond.

Ronnie glanced over the shop then said to Burt and Grady. "Y'all heard about that sonofabitch Larry?"

Larry's smirk faded. Burt tried not to look at him, afraid he might be mesmerized by the sight of the impossible man, like gazing at a solar eclipse.

"Yeah, we heard," Grady said. "Car accident, right?"

"A big, beautiful car accident!" Ronnie had a perfectly cropped afro and wore a heavy gold chain, proudly sporting the style of another era. He held up his hands in a gesture of mock surprise, then pointed at the ceiling. "Hallelujah, praise heaven above! That asshole got all jacked up in a car wreck! Couldn't have happened to a nicer fella. Right, Burt?"

Burt broke a smile. "*You* said that. I didn't."

"Too soon?" Ronnie asked.

"Not for that guy," Grady added.

They laughed together, but Burt not as loudly as the others.

Larry fumed. Burt could feel it. He tried to push it from his mind as he built Ronnie's lunch.

"Man, I heard it was a bad one, too," Ronnie said.

Grady looked up. "Really?"

"Yeah, course you can't count on the news to report something like that. Got hit by some sort of fuel truck. Heard his Caddy caught on fire with him inside it. Shit, if the fire department woulda left him alone that fat motherfucker woulda burned for days, all that blubber just like candle wax.

"*Daaaaammn,*" Grady said.

Burt let his gaze wander anywhere but where Larry sat stuffing his face. "Maybe it was karma. Been stealing from us for years. Calling it protection. Protection from who?" This was a conversation he and Ronnie had shared many times over the years, and repeating it made Burt's temper flare as always, strengthening his resolve for having done what he did.

"You know who," Ronnie said. "You don't pay 'em, they gonna bust out your windows and take your merch. You payin' *them* to protect you from *them.*"

Burt worked up a smirk of his own and shot it at Larry, making sure the fat man could see it before returning to his friend. "I *was* payin' him," Burt said. "But I ain't anymore."

"I hear that." Ronnie raised his palm, and Burt slapped him high-five over the counter.

Ronnie paid and took his order to go. On the way out the door he said, "You know Tweedle-Dum gonna show up any day wantin' his handout, right? We ain't in the clear yet."

"I know," Burt said. "Maybe karma will get him too."

The door closed. Grady asked his boss, "Who's Tweedle-Dum?"

Burt shook his head and wiped off the prep counter with a hand towel. "Larry's big brother Julian."

Grady frowned. "*Big* brother? Bigger than Larry?"

Burt nodded. "And meaner."

Grady appeared not to notice Larry's dry laughter coming from the end of the bar.

The Azalea family owned the Main Street Plaza that housed Burt's Sandwich Shop and Johnson Dry Cleaning. Rent was surprisingly reasonable, but the Azalea siblings were two-bit criminal bullies who stole at will from their mother's lease-holders under the pretense of providing security for the premises.

Everyone in town had heard the story of how Mr. Burnside, owner of the book store, one day refused to pay Julian the money he demanded. Later that week in the dead of night, someone smashed all his shop windows, stole money from the register and trashed thousands in merchandise. The incident went down as the town's most audacious case of burglary in years. Word had it that Burnside had been paying off the Azaleas ever since.

All the local business owners knew damn well the biggest criminal threat in Trapper Valley came from the two goons who claimed to be its bouncers. And the older Burt got, the more he hated being fleeced by the brothers. Somebody had to do something, so he had devised a plan.

But Larry's presence in the shop today had been no part of that plan.

"Hey boss," Grady said, pointing outside. "Does Julian look anything like that?"

A heap of a man wearing a white jacket pulled open the door and stepped into the shop. Well over six feet tall and half as big around, he wore dark sunglasses and had black hair pulled back tightly in a ponytail. As the door swung closed behind him, he cracked the knuckles of both hands and looked around the room. He showed no notice of his brother seated nearby.

"Burt," Julian said in a low, joyless tone. The smell of cheap cologne filled the store.

"Afternoon, Mr. Azalea." Burt knew his own voice sounded flat, but he found it impossible to give it the same cheery lift he saved for his normal customers.

Grady had become a statue at the drink machine, where he'd been reloading the ice.

"Back to work," Burt told him.

The kid blinked twice then climbed up a footstool and hoisted the ice bucket over the edge of the machine. The cubes cascaded down into the bin.

"What can I get for you?" Burt asked the customer.

Julian took a deep breath and exhaled through his nose. "You heard the news about my brother?"

Burt dropped his head. "Yes, sir. I'm sorry to hear that. My condolences to you and your family."

"Yep," Julian said. He smacked his lips and kept scouring the place through his shades as though conducting some sort of investigation. "You could say it's been a real bitch of a day."

Then he just stood there silently. Burt shifted his feet and said, "Well, I'm sure he'll be missed."

"Under the circumstances, I'll be assuming Larry's responsibilities," Julian said. "You can count on my services for all security concerns here at the plaza. I'm known for my diligence and thoroughness. You won't be disappointed, and you won't have shit to worry about insofar as the growing criminal element here in the Valley."

Burt fixed on his rack of condiments and said nothing, while the lobes of his ears grew hot and his fingers began to itch. The steely glares of both brothers bored into him from each side like spade bits. *Exactly how much did this bastard know about Larry's death?*

"I'm going to need all the twenties in your register," Julian said. "You keep the tens, fives and ones. You need change for your business this afternoon; I get that. I don't want you to think I'm a bad guy. But unfortunately the family's got some sudden expenses to cover. Funeral services and what-not."

Someone approached the door from the sidewalk. Burt recognized Club-Sandwich-Diet-Coke, but the young lady walked away after seeing Julian's monstrous frame looming inside.

Without a word, Burt stepped over to the register and pressed the button marked *No Sale*. The drawer shot open. Grady shrank back into the stock area, out of Julian's sight. Burt collected the bills from the twenties compartment, folded them and handed over the stack. Julian slipped it into his coat pocket.

As he did this, Larry snickered from the corner. "See, old man? The show must go on."

Burt bit the inside of his cheek and said to Julian, "Anything else I can get you?"

The bigger Azalea scanned the menu on the wall. "Yeah. Matter of fact, let me try one of those chili dogs my brother was always prattling on about."

Burt set his jaw to one side and cast a glance at Larry. "I'll be happy to."

The dead man's eyelids narrowed to coin slots. The vertical crease in his brow deepened like a knife wound. He swallowed a mouthful of food and said, "Don't even think about it…"

Pulling the silver spice shaker from the pocket of his apron, Burt placed it in the row of other condiments. He forked a frank onto the hot griddle where it popped and hissed.

Larry tugged at his collar and darted his head at his brother. "Jules," he said. "Julian!"

His brother stood smugly with his arms crossed, inspecting the sandwich-making process. Burt had learned long ago, however, that once he slid the food to the back of the counter, the customer lost sight of it behind the half-wall partition. That's where he applied a liberal helping of Top Secret Spice Mix to Julian Azalea's hotdog.

"It's poison, Jules!" Larry warned, voice rising. "Same shit he gave to me!"

Julian never flinched, only studied the thick, steaming chili Burt ladled onto his order. He licked his lips.

"Don't eat it!" Larry raged. He grew red with anger. Literally.

Burt slid Julian the footlong and fries, bagged and ready to go. From the corner of his eye, he saw Larry's hair lick into yellow flames.

"Much obliged," Julian said from behind his impenetrable black lenses. He took the order, tipped his head and strode out of the shop.

A bright flash exploded from the end of the counter. "Nooooo!" Larry roared at his oblivious brother. The whole store shook, and Burt could no longer wrench his gaze from the blazing nightmare. Fire engulfed Larry's body as he grabbed the top of the plexi and pulled himself up from the stool.

Burt staggered backward into the potato-chip rack.

Orange flame whipped about the dead man's head like a hellish crown. His oily hair curled up, whitened and withered. The flesh of his face cracked and blistered. The ceiling tiles above him darkened and warped.

"Gonna tear you apart, old man!" The burning man's voice gurgled as if boiled in oil. The fabric of his clothes peeled back with spreading holes. "Gonna pull out your eyes. Gonna slice you open and peel off your face…"

Burt's limbs went rigid with stony panic. Fire and smoke flooded the store in a dizzying swirl. Reeling, falling, Burt hit his knees and gripped the apron across his chest. His heart raced with a thump against his knuckles—that galloping pulse he felt distinctly—yet he detected no wafting heat.

The flaming Larry hoisted a foot atop the bar stool and pushed up his smoldering girth onto the clear, hard plastic of the sneeze-shield, smearing it with cooked remnants of himself. One fiery arm groped over the edge, clutching the air between him and Burt. A swath of melting skin drooped loosely from the flab of his bicep. The flesh of his other palm stretched like liquid cheese where it stuck to the plexi.

"We'll flay you apart every day. All. Day. Long." Larry's eyes burst like ruptured yolks and leaked down his blackened cheeks.

Burt knew he should be pouring sweat, recoiling from the heat, but only deep cold gripped his guts. The smoke should be choking him blind, but instead he breathed freely. So Burt stood up. And he saw clearly that the hotdog he'd made for the dead man, the one Larry had been shoving into his face, lay untouched on the counter where he had first placed it.

He shot Larry an icy stare and snarled, "Then come and get me!"

Larry lifted his rippling face and froze.

"You can't, can you? You can't do *shit!*" Burt continued. "Because you're not *here!* You're … you're an *apparition!*" No heat. No smell. No eaten sandwich. Burt was a practical guy—to run a business required it—and he figured if ghosts could actually wreak bloody revenge, then the world would always be knee-deep in ravaged bodies. But that wasn't reality. That sort of thing didn't happen; murder simply wasn't in a ghost's wheelhouse.

It was, however, in *his*.

Larry stopped advancing and only perched there, burning.

Burt's growing confidence gave an edge to his voice. "I was right! You can't do a damn thing but intimidate. Trying to *scare* an old man."

"A *murderer!*" Larry croaked, barely intelligible.

Burt stared him down and made a concrete decision. He may have given into fear and intimidation while the Azalea brothers were alive, but there's no way in hell he would tolerate it in their death. "I ain't having a heart attack today, if that's what you were counting on. Nor a stroke. So, get out of my store."

Larry gave a hiss like meat in a skillet.

"Now!" Burt said.

The man's charred face twisted with rage. "We'll be waiting for you. Both of us will. You'll be ours when the time comes."

Burt inhaled a deep breath and took a long stride toward the burning man. He stuck out his chest. "If I end up where you're at, you won't have to wait. I'll come for *you.*"

Larry leered silently for a moment then gave a snide laugh. He lowered himself from the countertop. He ran his fingers through the flames on his scalp, slicking them back. Slowly he walked down the lobby. He was gone before he made it to the door.

The store felt as empty as it had ever been. Burt placed fingers to his temples and worried about the gray matter that had always served him well until today.

"Are you okay?"

Grady's voice snatched him back to planet earth, as it seemed to do more and more often these days. Burt turned to find the young man holding two new racks of bread loaves, with his mouth hitched to one side, visibly worried.

Burt cleared his throat and straightened his apron. "How long you been standing there?"

Grady swallowed. "Long enough to see you have a really weird conversation with nobody."

Burt quickly busied himself with the minutiae of running the store, straightening the condiments and wiping down the prep table. "Yeah, well … never mind that. Senior moment, I guess."

Grady's brow arched a little higher. "Burt, you sure you're okay?"

Hamburger-Mustard-Onions walked into the store with her young daughter, Grilled-Cheese. A welcomed distraction. They both approached the counter with bright smiles.

Burt turned to Grady and said, "I'm fine. Really. Now, come on. We've got customers. Time to get busy."

Grady, always the diligent employee, did as he was told.

Burt appreciated a strong work ethic and decided to give the kid an hourly raise. He'd like him to stick around. They had a lot of sandwiches to make.

Waist Deep

"Your turn, Mikey." Butch extended the knife, handle first. "Get him in the throat. Finish him off."

Saliva pooled beneath Mikey's tongue at the nauseating thought of slicing into the old man's neck. He took a step backward and shook his head. "No. I can't. Y'all do it."

Mr. Finley sat duct-taped to the chair. His head hung forward on his bony frame, undershirt drenched with sweat and blood. He wheezed and shuddered with every breath.

Big Hank, all six-foot-six and four-hundred pounds of him, took a step forward into the light. "Like hell," he said to Mikey. "We're in this together. Now take the damned knife."

Mikey closed his eyes. Like on *Star Trek* he wanted to beam right out this place and be magically transported home, or anywhere else. Tonight, he and the others had chased their hate to the point of no return. Hank had been the first to carve on Mr. Finley. Then Butch had taken his pound of flesh. Now, if Mikey refused the knife, he'd break their trust, and Hank and Butch were two men he did not want as enemies. Not tonight. Not out here in the middle of nowhere.

"Take it," Butch said with an edge to his voice, waggling the knife. He had wiry black hair and one gold tooth right in front, next to all the yellow ones.

Mikey wrapped his fingers around the rusty carving knife and brought it up for inspection. Solidly constructed with a full tang running through the wooden handle, the serrated blade glistened in the dim lamplight with a maroon sheen of blood.

Mikey gritted his teeth. Sometimes you just had to rip off the Band-Aid. With a grunt, he whirled around and drove the full ten inches of steel into Finley's side. The man buckled and moaned.

"How you like *that!*" growled Big Hank.

Mikey reeled backward and puked onto the rotted floorboards of the rickety shack. He wanted to show the other two he meant business while actually missing any vital organs. But he knew he'd never shake off the feeling of pushing the blade into the old man's flesh.

Butch whapped the side of Finley's head and spat into his thin gray hair. "You need to go ahead and die, you sick ol' fuck, if you know what's good for you."

Big Hank's stubbly face hitched into a sneer. He towered over Finley and bent down just inches from his ear to whisper: "That's right. You better cash out, you ol' pervert. 'Cause the state you're in right now is as good as it's ever gonna get for you again."

Hank grabbed the knife, ripped it out and drove it back in. Finley's skinny shoulders seized up for an instant then sank lower along with his head.

"I didn't do it," the old man muttered.

A long sigh escaped his mouth as he slowly expired, like the final hiss of a flattening tire. At last he went silent and still.

Butch grabbed an open can of Budweiser from the floor and slammed down three heavy gulps. Beer trickled down the corners of his mouth. He closed his eyes and pressed the can to his sweating forehead.

Hank wiped his hands on his overalls and paced the shack in a circle, the wood creaking beneath him. "Fuck that old bastard.

Good riddance. Won't be gettin' his hands on any more little boys now, will he?"

Butch took another swig and said, "No, sir. He sure won't."

Mikey's head swam with booze and adrenaline and two torturous kinds of fear. He feared discovery, because his actions tonight made him a murderer, vital organs or not. And he feared the truth, because they'd just killed a fellow townie, a man they'd known their entire lives, based on the unsubstantiated claims of Hank's 13-year-old brother.

"I reckon we oughtta do something about the body," Butch said.

Hank stopped pacing. He lifted his ball cap and scratched his scalp, tapping his thumb against his thigh while studying Finley's corpse.

"You think the gators would eat him," Butch said, "if we drug him into the swamp?"

Hank nudged the dead man's shin with the toe of his boot. "That's just what I was wonderin'."

"I don't think that's a good idea," Mikey said. The other two jerked their heads around like they'd forgotten he was in the room. "I mean, what if no gators show up?"

Hank and Butch exchanged a glance. Both red-faced and bleary-eyed, they were far from thinking clearly.

"Or, what if the gators show, but they don't finish off the body?" Mikey said. "I mean, he's got knife wounds all through him. Probably got our DNA dripping off him. He ends up in a murder investigation, we all might end up in jail."

Hank closed his eyes and shook his head like he was disappointed with Mikey's concerns. Butch only frowned. They'd never appreciated his suggestions back at the cabinet shop, and it appeared the same held true when it came to concealing a crime.

"I think the gators is the way to go," Hank said.

"Me too," Butch said.

Mikey's stomach rolled over. The decision had been made right then and there, and he knew no further discussion on the subject would be tolerated. As Hank cut Finley from the chair, Mikey realized he had only one course of action: To hope for a hungry gator.

***

Mikey pulled his beat-up Celica next to the trailer after midnight. All the lights were out, which meant Lyla was probably out cold in the bed. He crept into the house to avoid waking her or the baby. He needed a shower. Not only to clean himself up, but also to clear his mind, to let the hot water rinse away the fog of booze and confusion so he could plan his way out of this mess. He eased the sagging screen door closed so it wouldn't pop loudly behind him. He shut the front door, enveloping himself in total darkness, and locked the deadbolt. Two steps into the house and he tripped over an unseen object, catching himself on the wall. "Dammit!"

With a click the room brightened. He saw a stuffed pony tangled between his feet. Lyla, sprawled on the couch and squinting, had her fingers on the pull chain of the end-table lamp.

"You're home awful damn late," she said.

She looked at the blood on his shirt. He looked at it, too. A red handprint smeared across his belly—his own handprint from wiping it clean.

"What the hell have you gotten into?"

"Fishin'. Been fishin'."

"Yeah, right."

"Ain't you ever heard of night fishin'?"

"I ain't never heard of *you* night fishing."

He unbuttoned the beige work shirt, working from the top down, and peeled it off his shoulders.

"You need a shower before you get in bed."

"Planned on it," he said.

"Who was you with? I been calling your phone."

His mobile phone—he hadn't noticed it missing. That modern necessity, that ever-present lifeline of communication which had become as standard an accessory as his socks and skivvies, had disappeared at some point throughout the night.

He cut a glance at her, and the way her jaw set to one side told him she wouldn't like the answer no matter who he said he'd been with.

"Big Hank and Butch."

She muttered something he couldn't make out and then said, "I didn't think you liked them much. I didn't think they liked you much, either."

"They're co-workers, Lyla. And something happened today. Something bad. Hank was pretty upset. So me and Butch took him out for some drinks."

"I can imagine," she said. "I can smell it on you from here."

That hot shower was looking better than ever.

"Besides," she said. "I done heard about Hank's brother. What's his name? Ethan?"

"Evan."

"Evan, then. Gladys told me all about it at the salon. Word's all over town."

The memory flashed through his mind, ugly and painful. "I was there today, Lyla. When it happened."

"Oh my god," she said, voice softening. "It happened at the shop?"

"I was cutting plywood." Mikey gazed out the window into the night. "I turned off the table saw. The motor quit buzzing, and that's when we heard the screaming."

Henry Dawson, known around Dusky Cove as "Big Hank", co-owned and operated Dawson Cabinetry, having had come into possession after an infamous family squabble led to his father's disappearance. The nature of the fight, exactly which family members had been involved, and the fate of his father all remained a mystery among Hank's friends and co-workers. When asked if his dad was dead, Hank would predictably reply with "to me, he is" and then make perfectly clear that the subject was strictly off-limits for conversation.

By virtue of location—outside the city limits and beyond the reach of municipal zoning codes—the Dawsons lived and worked on the same plot of land. Hank, Evan and their mother resided in a modest single-story house next to the cabinet shop.

The day had begun like a thousand others, with a stack of four-by-eight veneered plywood and a rack of inch-thick oak stock for fabricating face-frames and cabinet components. The compressor roared to life, the air guns started popping, and Mikey went to work cutting the boards to spec as the smell of sawdust filled the air. Hank assembled the carcasses, while Butch routed the door panels and cut dovetails for the drawers.

Evan, on summer vacation from school, usually showed up in the afternoons to finish-sand the furniture then apply the wood stain and polyurethane topcoats. Unlike his mammoth older brother, the boy was gentle, polite and soft-spoken with a slight build and a face that Butch had once described as "almost pretty."

Fifteen minutes before lunch, Mikey completed a rip on a cabinet panel, hit the saw switch and watched the blade stop spinning as the shrill whine of the engine faded away. The sound was replaced with a faint human cry from somewhere outdoors. Curious, Mikey stepped to the window, and the voice grew louder. The person sounded familiar, but panicked and screaming.

"You hear that?" he called across the workshop to Hank and Butch.

Hank reached over to the radio humming on his bench and turned down the volume on the country music. The scream became clearer, sounded nearer—right outside.

"Hank! Mom! Ohhhh Gaawwwwwd! Help me, somebody!"

Hank dropped his nail gun. The hose slid through his hand to the ground. He took flight for the door, knocking over a chair, dashing with impressive speed for such a huge man. Mikey looked at Butch, and they both followed suit.

Outside the door, Hank stopped in his tracks. Evan staggered toward them, blood covering his crotch and legs. His face, ghostly pale and contorted with horror, bobbled on his shoulders as he stumbled closer.

"Holy shit!" Butch said.

At the sound of his voice, Hank shot into motion. He rushed to the kid and scooped him up, cradling his slender frame. Mikey got closer and realized the boy was naked from the waist down, and something was missing.

"Call 911!" Hank said.

"Call 'em, Mikey!" Butch said, "I'll go get some towels!" He bolted for Hank's house.

Mikey dialed the emergency line on his phone.

Hank worked on Evan with his hands shaking like a palsy patient. The kid had quit screaming and gone limp in his brother's arms, eyes rolling back in his head. With his large sausage fingers, Hank tried to pinch closed the stump of Evan's severed penis, which was spurting blood in jets. He hadn't much left to work with.

"Spring clamp!" he shouted at Mikey. "Get me a spring clamp!"

Mikey looked at his phone. The call had dropped. Shitty, rural cell service.

He rushed into the workshop. One of the black plastic clamps held a miter joint together on Butch's bench. He ripped it off and shot back outside. Hank took it, squeezed it open and pinched closed Evan's cut-off member as the kid squealed with pain.

At least it was a sign of life.

"No time for an ambulance," Hank said. "Lost too much blood. Help me carry him to the truck."

Butch showed up with the towels, and they loaded Evan into the crew cab. Everyone blazed down the road to the emergency room with the kid shaking and blubbering.

"Mr. Finley!" Evan bawled. "It was him who did it, Hank! He's the one who cut me!"

***

"Finley?" Lyla said. "That old man lives up the dirt road behind the cabinet shop?"

"Yeah, that weird ol' coot always creeps around the woods at night."

"He said Finley done it?"

"What he told us." Mikey stood in the living room wearing only his briefs, holding his dirty clothes and ready for that shower.

"Baloney. Mr. Finley's the only one night-fishing," Lyla said. "That old man's harmless. My daddy knew him and said he was okay. Besides, that ain't the story Gladys told me."

Mikey glared at his wife. "What do you mean 'story Gladys told you'?"

"Gladys told me the Dawson boy was feeding the sheriff a whole different story than what you're telling. Blaming that fairy kid, Horton."

Daniel Horton was the most outspoken gay rights advocate the town had ever seen. The first out-of-the-closet homosexual at the local high school, Horton had founded the school's Gay-Straight Alliance which, the way Mikey heard it, consisted of two members—Horton and a militant feminist. The kid wrote controversial op-eds for the local newspaper, bashing the conservative community for being backwards and insensitive, and had started an internet blog that inspired many of the local youth to embrace his "progressive" point of view. This all gave the Dusky Cove Baptists a serious case of heartburn, but Mikey doubted that Danny Horton was capable of mutilating another person. In fact, he had an inkling that the kid's shock value was what made him an easy target as a scapegoat. Just like weird old Mr. Finley.

The curtains parted in Mikey's mind to reveal a sick suspicion: Evan was choosing people the community feared or hated, and blaming them for his missing dick.

Mikey's stomach flip-flopped like he'd eaten something rotten—digesting the notion that he'd helped kill an innocent man.

After leaving Evan in the care of the medics and his mom, they'd all partaken in a lot of liquor and vows of vengeance. Eventually Hank's blood had boiled to the point that he decided to walk the walk. He had Butch's full support, and Mikey had been stupid enough to tag along. They'd found Mr. Finley at dusk, bent over a patch of soil in his backyard, tending garden behind the ramshackle shotgun building he called a home. Hank had socked him in the back of the head, laid him out cold, then tossed the old man over his shoulder like a sack of potatoes. He chucked him in the back of the pickup, and forty minutes later they all arrived at Hank's fishing shack, which became the scene of the crime.

A loud pounding came from the trailer's front door. The baby started crying from the bedroom. Lyla cursed and stomped off to check on their daughter. Mikey opened the door to find Butch standing there holding a Budweiser.

"We got problems," Butch said.

***

Neither of them were fit to drive, but Butch tore down the road while pounding beer on the way to Hank's place. Mikey, who gripped the door handle as they sped along, explained his prevailing theory about Evan's lies.

Butch twisted up his face and said, "What are you talkin' about, son? Who the hell cuts off their own pecker?"

Mikey turned up his palms. "Who knows? I guess somebody who doesn't want to be a guy anymore."

Butch pondered this and did not argue the point, nor did he seem particularly troubled by the prospect of having killed the wrong man. Then again, his eyes were beginning to cross. "Ain't none of that matter now. We got bigger fish to fry."

Mikey winced. Any news that overshadowed the murder of Mr. Finley would have to be absolutely horrific in scope, and if that was the case, Mikey simply did not want to hear about it. He wanted to go far away from Dusky Cove and never look back. He'd send for his wife and kid.

But Mikey knew the sour truth. He was already stuck waist-deep in the mire and didn't have the option to run.

"I got a call," Butch said. "Hank's done caught up with that Horton fairy."

"What?"

"I gotta give it to him," Butch shook his head admiringly. "The man does act fast."

"What the hell are you talking about?" Mikey realized his voice was screeching with a note of terror, and Butch gave him a disgusted look.

"He's got him at his place right now. We gotta go help him wrap this whole thing up."

"Wrap it up!"

"Yes, wrap it up. We're all in this together."

"I ain't killing nobody else!"

"I don't think you're gonna have to. Pretty sure Hank's got it handled."

"For the love of God!"

"Don't fag out on us now, Mikey! If Hank gets pegged for murder, who you think they're gonna come after next? We got to hide it all, man. We got to make it all disappear tonight like we was never involved."

Mikey had the sensation of slowly sinking into a bog, fighting for the bank but being sucked deeper into the muck with every struggling motion. He sank under the surface, and the vision went gray then black, hazily replaced with a courtroom, two rows of jurors, twelve angry faces, zooming out of focus. Prison bars slammed closed before him with a cold metal clang.

"I can't do it," Mikey said.

Butch laughed without a trace of humor. "You ain't got a choice."

***

Butch's Malibu slowed as they approached the cabinet shop and the Dawson house. The trees thinned as they rounded a bend, and Mikey saw an unfamiliar vehicle, an old, blocky Cadillac, parked in the house driveway. Hank's truck was there, too. The house's front door opened, and a large figure bounded down the steps. With long blonde hair and a flowing gown, this mountain of a woman carried a rifle in one hand and stormed toward the workshop.

Butch slumped down in his seat and kept the car at a steady cruise as they rolled past, peering out the window. "Shit!" he said after driving a short distance.

"Who was that?"

"Hell if I know!" Butch's chin jutted out. His chest heaved. He punched the steering wheel twice, hard, then winced and shook his open fingers in the air. "Godammit! What else can go wrong?"

The tank in the dress was not Hank's mother. Butch had said Mrs. Dawson was staying at the hospital with Evan.

"That Horton's mom, you think?" Mikey said.

"Maybe," Butch said. "Don't matter. She's got a gun. We can't just sit and do nothing."

A turn came up. Butch hit the brakes and skid into a U-turn, slinging Mikey into the door. With a punch of the gas and a squeal of rubber, they shot back in the direction they'd come.

Mikey blew a breath between his teeth, steaming that Butch never thought five feet ahead in life. "Exactly! Whoever it is, they got a gun, damn it! I don't plan on getting shot!"

"*Shhhh!*" Butch hissed as he killed the headlights, slowing the car to a creep as the house neared on the right. The cabinet shop lights burned bright like the whole operation was up and running in the dead of night.

Just off the road, at the top of the downhill gravel driveway, Butch pulled the car into park. He stopped the engine and jerked on the emergency brake. The familiar buzz of power equipment hummed through the windows of the workshop.

Butch pulled out a pack of Camels, shuffled one out and lit it. He looked at Mikey and must have read his expression. "I gotta settle my nerves, damn it," he said with a puff of smoke.

Mikey rubbed the bridge of his nose, trying to distance himself from the headache that had begun to throb behind his eyes. He pulled open the car door and stepped outside. He needed air. Butch joined him.

"I got a thirty-eight in the trunk," Butch said.

"That ain't a good idea."

"Shut up." Butch retrieved the gun and lowered the trunk closed.

A rabble of raised voices brimmed through the ring of machinery as they neared the shop. The shouts were fierce and agitated, angry men cursing and bellowing.

Mikey looked at Butch who thumbed at the center window, the one not blocked by a supply cabinet or cluttered by a drill press. Sneaking like burglars, they gathered just beneath the window and raised up in tandem, peeking over the sill through the dusty glass.

Inside the workshop, the lady hulk stood at least as tall as Big Hank. With her back to the window, her entire frame trembled along with the rifle in her hands, which was aimed straight at their employer and co-conspirator.

Someone else lay bound to the table top of the radial arm saw. Restrained by layered straps of heavy duct tape, this person of a thinner build bled from many open wounds and squirmed at the hands and feet—the only moveable parts. Wood chisels and screwdrivers protruded from his sides and limbs like surgical instruments. Some sort of rag partially concealed the boy's face, gagging his mouth, but Mikey could tell from the fancy hairdo that it was Danny Horton on the chopping block.

"Lord have mercy," Butch whispered. "Hank's gonna split that kid right up the middle."

The ten-inch circular blade of a radial arm saw glides along an overhead track for making long rips and plunge cuts in woodwork. The boy had been taped down spread-eagle to the extension table with the spinning blade directed right at his crotch. Hank, wearing his customary gray overalls like any other day at work, loomed over him with one hand on the saw lever while staring at the gun the woman pointed at him. Mikey knew that with a drop of the lever and a quick shove of the cutting head, Danny Horton would suddenly have much longer legs.

Butch motioned to the front door and crept around the corner of the building.

Mikey stayed frozen in place. Tonight had most likely ruined his life. Already tangled in a web of fuck-ups and bad luck, the last thing he needed was to make another wrong move.

"Drop the gun, lady!" Butch's voice wavered like a warped record.

Mikey returned to the window to see Butch standing in the doorway, revolver raised with both hands and pointed at the woman. Butch advanced inside with two stumbling steps, and Mikey realized that in his inebriated state the guy might even miss the ground if he didn't aim hard.

Hank scowled at Butch. "Go on, get outta here, Butch. This don't involve you."

The big woman stood her ground, the barrel's aim stuck on Hank.

"Hell it don't!" Butch yelled. "I ain't going to jail, Hank! Now, drop the gun, lady, or I swear I'll shoot!"

Danny Horton whipped his head around, looking wild-eyed and trying to plead for mercy through the wad of dirty cloth crammed down his mouth.

"You let that boy loose, Hank!" The command thundered out of the lady in a gruff bass-heavy voice, and Mikey fixed on her frame. Her shoulders looked twice as broad as his own, her hands the size of thick winter gloves.

"I ain't letting him go," Hank shouted over the buzz of the saw. His dirty ballcap hung low over his face, but when he would lift his head into the light Mikey could see his eyes—cold, distant and unhinged. "I'm gonna do the same thing to this queer that he did to Evan. And nobody's gonna stop me."

"Evan did it to himself," the lady said. "And you know that. You drove him to do it, you hateful bastard!"

"Shut up." Hank said. "That ain't true."

"Just like you drove me away. Drove me away from my family!"

"Shut up!"

"Because you can't accept people for who they are."

"I said *shut up!*" Hank growled, and the saw buzzed.

Butch closed in, and when he faced the lady his jaw fell open.

"You can't accept people for who they are, so you hate them," she said. "Just like you hate yourself for who *you* are. Who you *really* are, deep down. The person you're afraid to admit being."

"*Shut the fuck up!*" Hank roared, baring teeth.

"Anybody caught you in your panties and mini skirt, Hank? Anybody other than *me*? You shared your secret with the world yet, or you just a coward and a bigot?"

With a jerk of Hank's elbow the blade fell into place between Horton's knees, the fin of a shark savoring its first bite. "I hate you."

"Don't do it!" she said.

The saw ripped forward, plunging a red trench through the groin of the squirming teenager, who bucked and howled through his gag.

"*Nooooooo!*" The lady's rifle trembled then jerked up at the ceiling. She blasted a round into the roof and brayed like a wounded animal. She cocked it and shot the rafters again, then cast aside the gun which skittered across the floor. She threw herself onto a workbench and covered her face. Her body shuddered with sobs.

Butch shrunk against the far wall, the thirty-eight at his side and his free hand clutching at his mouth.

Hank, his overalls now splattered with vibrant gore, stalked to the supply closet twelve feet away and ripped open the door. He lifted out a chainsaw. They kept the 24-inch Stihl for those rare occasions when a property owner had a felled walnut or cherry for harvest. Hank tugged on the pull-cord.

Mikey raced around to the entrance and dashed inside the shop. On seeing the kid split open, the world felt foreign, gauzy and unreal. He considered his numbness might be what doctors called shock. That, or booze-soaked panic. He knew but one thing: Get Butch and run.

"Come on, damn it!" he shouted at Butch.

The lady looked up and, as Mikey had expected, had a shadow of whiskers and a prominent Adam's apple. Hank's long-lost daddy. He'd gotten the call about Evan. To make the drive within a day, he must not have been lost very far away.

Hank jerked on the pull-start, and the saw rumbled for a second. He pumped the choke.

"Hank's lost it!" Mikey said. "Butch, he might just kill us all."

"Yeah," Hank said. "I'm going to."

Butch's lips were moving but no words formed. He stared at the dead teenager and didn't budge. Mikey clenched his teeth and ran over to him. He grabbed Butch by the shirt and shook him. "Snap out of it!"

Butch blinked rapidly.

At the other end of the workshop, Hank cranked the chainsaw to life with a hellish buzz and set his sights on his father.

"Don't do this," the elder Dawson said. He faced his son and took a step for the rifle on the floor, but Hank gunned the saw and advanced. His father retreated, stumbling in his high-heels. He reached down, plucked off his pumps and tucked them beneath his arm.

The smell of the chainsaw's exhaust filled the room. Mikey knew the jagged spinning blade had all the power to rip logs to ribbons; flesh and bone were nothing.

Hank licked his gums and flared his nostrils. Then he snarled and stalked forward. Mr. Dawson turned and ran. Mikey snatched Butch by the shirt sleeve. They both took flight and beat Hank's dad out the door, sprinting uphill for the car. Hank roared and charged, and Mikey dared not look back.

A human profile moved in a lit window across the street. The neighbors had been wakened by the commotion.

Mikey made it to the Malibu first and flung open the driver's door.

Butch chugged up right behind him. "This is my ride!" He wore his keys on a belt loop of his jeans, and Mikey snatched them off.

"Shut up," Mikey said, diving into the car.

Butch shot over to the passenger door. "Go, go, go!" he said, climbing inside.

With teeth chattering, Mikey jangled through the arsenal of keys on the ring. "Which one!"

Butch leaned over to sort through the clutter.

Mikey realized the chainsaw's rumble had taken a different turn. Mr. Dawson hadn't followed them. With Hank on his heels, he'd run for the Caddy parked at the house some twenty yards away. He hadn't made it.

Blood sprayed in a fan as Hank stood over his father and grinded the saw through his torso, slashing in every direction. Like a kid playing in a sandbox, his movements were brash and enthusiastic, slinging pieces of his old man across the lawn this way and that.

The roar of the chainsaw died to an idle purr. Mikey heard sirens in the distance.

Spit pooled beneath his tongue once again as he watched Hank bend down and take the dripping blonde wig off Mr. Dawson's head. Hank then pulled off his baseball hat and put on the wig, its curly locks bouncing on his thick shoulders.

Butch pointed to a key with a naked lady on the fob. "It's that one! Now drive like hell!"

Mikey grabbed the key, sunk it in and cranked the engine. He hit the gas, but the tires spun in place.

Hank knelt down and dipped his fingertips in his father's wounds. He brought the hand to his face.

"Let's go, let's go!" Butch shouted.

"We're stuck!" Mikey pegged the gas, but the tires would not reverse up the gravel incline onto the road.

Hank angled his head in their direction. A deranged smile stretched across his face, the grinning lips a fresh wet crimson. The saw buzzed back to life with a spray of smoky exhaust, and he headed for their car.

"Hurry up, dammit!"

Mikey jammed the gearshift and shot forward down the driveway. He cut a sharp right, and the car spun around in the front yard. Hank lunged at them, slicing with fury. The blade banged off the passenger side as Butch screamed in a high warble. The rear end fishtailed. Mikey fought with the steering. Butch hugged the dashboard as the car bounced and ramped up the hill of the rocky lawn. With a vault and a jarring landing, they bounded onto the blacktop.

Sirens grew louder. Mikey looked back to see the blue-red glow of cop cars coming around the bend.

Hank, brandishing the saw, trudged up the bank and onto the road. He bent over and appeared to catch his breath. Then he came charging right at them.

But Hank shrank away. The Malibu roared, and Mikey watched in the rearview mirror as the road unreeled between them and the madman. As they sped away, multiple police vehicles swarmed around Hank and his bloody chainsaw.

Big Hank was going to have a hell of a lot of explaining to do.

***

At long last, the hot water from his shower at home splashed over Mikey like summer sunshine. It lapped across his skin, warming him like a cozy blanket wrapped by a mother around her young. He hugged his arms, trying to heat the cold that remained within him despite the superficial comfort. He was rotten inside and knew it.

Delirious, skull cracking from DTs and hours of sheer terror, Mikey hung his head. The suds dripped with the runoff and swirled down the drain. Yesterday he had considered himself a decent human being, a live-and-let-live kind of guy who meant no harm to anyone—just like old Mr. Finley probably meant no harm. The old man had simply kept to himself and in return people treated him like he was strange, different ... disposable. Mikey knew that's why it had been so much easier to go after Finley during their self-righteous stupor than it ever would have been to murder anyone else. Now he was guilty of the worst of all sins, and all at the behest of a maniac who got his marching orders from a troubled young liar.

Through all the soap and shampoo, Mikey's self-loathing lingered with him like the stink of a dead dog.

Still feeling dirty, he laid down in bed next to his snoring wife. The alarm clock read 4:30 AM, and he was scheduled to work at seven. But he supposed the office would be closed today, anyway. He wondered how long it would take before the police came knocking, asking their questions. He also wondered if the gators had gotten around to eating Finley's body ... or if they ever would.

And he tried to remember where in hell he'd left his damned cell phone.

Louise, Your Shed's On Fire

I'd love a nice cup of coffee, but a steaming cup of hot black sludge is what sits on the table in front of me. All I could find in the pantry was Herb's half pouch of ground French roast, which tastes a lot like regular coffee but with a heaping scoop of cigarette ash. Don't ask me why the French would come up with something so disgusting, but I need the pick-me-up if I'm going to get these meaty thighs into motion.

That's how Herb had described them. "Meaty." I don't think he was trying to be mean, but it never made me feel good when he said things like that.

Last week Herb broke things off with me and moved into the condo of his old flame, Hillary Belton, nicknamed "Thrillary" back in high school. She'd swollen up since their first breakup, but then lap-band surgery slimmed her down again, and now she has thinner thighs than me. I'd say *good for her*, but I don't really want anything good for her. Forgive me, Jesus.

Besides, there's still a few available men my age around town. A couple of them, anyway. I think.

My plan is to get in shape by dancersizing to the *Leighton Emerson Body-Burn* DVD that's playing on the TV. No more meaty thighs for Meg Thatcher. Well, maybe a little meaty because I've always been a muscular woman and never had the longest legs. But dadgum it, they won't be fat. Leighton and I are going to make sure of that. "Right, Porkchop?"

My Siberian Husky is sitting on the floor beside me. Porkchop looks up and tilts his head at me like he's not fully convinced. It's his signature look. I pet him anyway and take a sip of the coffee.

Gag. Even when mixed with sugar and whole milk, it still tastes like mud, so I hold my nose and chug it down like a teenager drinking cheap wine. I've gotta get it in gear since I'm due for my breakfast shift at the diner in an hour.

From my seat at the table, I see a light surging through the window. With dawn breaking at half past five, the sky is still a deep blue-gray, and an orange glow shines not from the eastern horizon but from somewhere above my house. Is the roof on fire?

The yard grows brighter than in broad daylight. Porkchop starts barking. I jump up from my chair and then—*WHOOMP!* A huge thud hits outside with the crash of shattered glass. The shockwave shakes my house. The hardwood floor tickles the soles of my socked feet, and the ceramic chickens jingle on my collectibles shelf.

I'm pretty sure something fell from the sky, but I'm not sure I want to know what it is.

Who am I kidding? I run to the window and poke my head outside. The glow is gone and the sky is back to its normal dusky gray. Sunlight is peeking out across the hillside.

My nose tingles at the stink of something burning, and a swirl of thick smoke spirals up from the Tisdales' work shed next door. Not good.

I click the remote to pause the *Body Burn* DVD. Leighton Emerson's rock-hard physique freezes on screen with her one leg extended in a "pistol squat," which looks way too difficult for me to attempt anyway.

I phone Louise Tisdale on speed-dial. She's an elderly woman whose kids have recently moved her husband to a nursing home on account of his dementia. I keep tabs on her in case she needs help with anything. Louise is a fellow early-riser, so it worries me when she doesn't answer, but her hearing gets worse all the time. She might not have heard the ring. I better make sure she knows a meteor wrecked her shed.

I put on my sneakers, drop a dog biscuit into Porkchop's bowl, and give him a quick ruffle behind the ears before stepping out back and closing the door. I catch a flash from the corner of my eye, and another deep thump echoes in the distance on the opposite side of my house. Meteor shower? Maybe a plane exploded. I see nothing in the sky but fading stars and scattered clouds.

A couple of flames lick up from the hole in Louise's shed roof, so I shuffle over to the Tisdales', open the screen and pound on their front door. It shakes ajar, and there's no time to waste, so I rush inside and barely give Louise a wave as she looks up from her knitting.

"You got a fire out back!" The kitchen's in the rear and it opens onto a deck through a sliding patio door. The lock flips open with a thumb switch. The door drags across the sill like the bearings are packed with sand, but I finally force it open and make it outside. Louise follows in her nightgown, but I'm already down the steps and cranking the hose bib on the rear wall. I grab the whole snaky coil of garden hose and race it to the shed, but it's all bundled up and jerks out of my arms. I go back and gather it from the ground, searching for the nozzle, fighting with the tangle. I'm getting soaked, and the flames are climbing higher.

At last I straighten out a loop and beeline it for the shed. The keychain is hanging in the lock, so I throw open the door and go about hosing the place down like I'm an old pro. Believe or not, the flames haven't spread too much. The shed is dark inside, except for

the fire, but I can see the burning ceiling joists just fine, so I soak
'em thoroughly. After a lot of hissing and steaming, everything
goes out.

By golly, I've saved the day.

I back out of the doorway, and Louise shimmies over to me in
her slippers. "Goodness gracious!" she says, "What in the world
happened?"

"A comet or something."

"A comet!"

"Or a meteor. I'm not sure yet."

We should probably call the police or an actual firefighter, but
being a curious sort I want to get first look at whatever came
crashing down from the heavens. In a quiet little town like ours,
nothing exciting ever happens. Given the rut my life's been in
lately, I'm not eager to give up this little taste of adventure just yet.

I cut a look at Louise. "I think we ought to investigate. What
do you think?"

She gives a nod and holds up a flashlight. "I'm with you."

Louise sticks it in my hand. I click on the beam, and she follows
right behind me.

The work-shed is an old two-car garage fronted by a couple of
overhead doors—the type that pull up by hand. The floor is made
of gravel, and instead of cars, the shed stores a rusty utility trailer,
a Craftsman riding mower, and a whole arsenal of Mr. Tisdale's
tools and machinery. The place is cramped with lumber shelving,
and since the lights got knocked out in the crash, dark shapes and
deep shadows crowd all around us. We can see the two-foot hole in
the roof, though, and something smoldering from dead center of
the shed floor.

"I guess you were right," Louise says, her breath tickling my
shoulder. "Looks like we got us a real live shooting star!"

I scoot around the front of the trailer so I can bend down and lift up the first garage door within reach. Silver light spills in from the morning. A lot of those shadows vanish, and some turn from black to gray.

A scuttling sound comes from the far corner. I shine the light, and the shadows bleed away. Could be anything; a spooked squirrel, a mouse, a rat (which I don't want near me). A *bang!* from our left gives me a start. The beam shines on a wall-mounted pegboard with all sorts of pliers and wrenches hanging from it. But no sign of any critters.

"Louise, y'all don't have a cat, do you?"

"Used to," she says. "Mr. Titties ran off a year ago."

I make a mental note to ask about the cat's name, and file it for later.

I hold my breath and move the light through the shed. Not sure why I'm so nervous. The rear wall is lined with a countertop cluttered with hand tools, jars of screws and cardboard boxes, all mysterious lumps until the flashlight hits them. I hear a rustle from the counter, then a small clattery crash at the floor level, like a bowl of nails spilling to the ground.

Louise squeezes my shoulder. "See any varmints?"

"Not yet," I tell her.

Nearing the crater in the shed floor, I peer at some sort of smoking stone a couple feet down that's split into two jagged round halves. With a shell about an inch thick, the hollow inside of the walls looks shiny, wet and inky.

"You think that's some kind of space egg?" Louise asks.

I think maybe she watches too many monster movies. Then I think maybe I don't watch enough, because something skitters across the wall right above the messy countertop. And I don't mean to ignore her question, but at that very moment my tongue is stuck to my teeth. I didn't get a good look, but it's no cat. More like a tumor. Black like the shadows, the glimpse I caught didn't really have a shape, but the squirmy way it moved—like nothing I've ever seen—gives me a deep chill.

"You saw it too..." Louise says, and I'm not sure if it's a statement or a question.

"I saw something. Don't know what."

She tugs on my tank top. "I think maybe we oughtta call the police."

Another racket, and I shoot the flashlight at the left rear corner. One of Mr. Tisdale's four-foot hand levels swings back and forth from a nail on the side wall.

"It's getting closer to us," Louise says. "I don't like this." Her fingers tremble and move to her chin.

Then she stares at something in the shed, and her mouth drops open. A black twisting thing springs at us from the darkness. I jump back and grab for Louise. She raises both hands, but the thing flies up and latches onto her and squeezes her hands against her face. She stumbles backward, the thing wrapping her with sticky tentacles like ribbons of tar.

A rake in the corner! I snatch it up and scrape at the black creature-thing with the leaf end so not to hit Louise with the stick. Between my raking and Louise wiggling around, the black thing shakes loose and plops to the ground but never quits moving. With eight or twelve swirling limbs, the thing's got a juicy black center like a spider or octopus but stays in a constant thrashing frenzy like that cartoon Tasmanian Devil.

"Smack it!" Louise hollers, so I rear back with the rake to give it a mighty wallop. The creature shoots away, and I miss as it scuttles up the wall. Must be coated in glue, the way it scrambles straight up the plywood like my brother's Wacky Wall-Walker from when we were kids. When it wriggles across the ceiling joists in our direction I quit watching and make a dash for the deck. Louise is right on my heels.

"Owww! Meg it's got me!"

I spin around, and Louise's face is stretched out in pure white terror. She spills onto the grass, and that black squirmy thing is clinging to her back. She screams louder than I thought her frail frame could muster, and then that scream deepens into a croak like a monster toad, and the creature's black juicy body deflates just like a balloon. The big bulbous thing shrinks right up, and all those spindly snake-legs shrivel up too, and everything sucks down into a tiny dark spot on Louise's back that I can see through her torn nightgown. The thing has injected itself into her.

I swoon and brace myself on the deck banister. *Oh poor Louise!* She'd never have been hurt if I hadn't been so foolish to investigate. I rush over to her, not exactly sure what I'd just seen.

Her body starts bucking like a bull. All her limbs kick and flail. I grab my hair. How do you stop a seizure? Do I stick something in her mouth so she doesn't swallow her tongue? Somebody help!

After a minute she stops on her own, lying face-down in the yard and completely still.

And then things get worse.

Louise breaks into a pitch-black sweat. The pores of her exposed skin leak out a dark fluid like dirty motor oil. First it beads up on the surface, then it runs and drips. And suddenly Louise bolts upright with more zip and quickness than I've ever seen from her.

But she ain't right. Even her eyes bubble with blackness. The inky liquid seeping from her face reminds me of Herb's French roast.

Louise parts her lips and lets out a mad-dog roar that turns my blood cold. Then she runs straight at me. Her right hand draws back like it's ready to swipe, and she's got really long nails. I dip to the right but she follows my dodge. Keeping within reach, she claws at my bare shoulder. I spin around and hurl her along with her weight so she goes careening away and topples to the ground.

The same thing happens to me. I lose my balance and drop onto my rump.

Louise is back up first. The black fluid masks her face, mats her hair and seeps through her gown. She snarls like an animal and charges me.

Don't do this, Louise!

She leaps off the ground. I roll onto my back. With unbelievable height, Louise soars like a black angel against the blue sky. But I draw back my legs. I curl them against me with the soles of my sneakers facing straight up. Louise comes down on me in a crazy rage, and I push up with my meaty thighs and catch her mid-section with a direct kick. The impact doubles her over and blasts air out her mouth. She launches back up and drifts to the side, where she thumps down to the ground and rolls against an azalea bush.

I'm looking up at a cloud, just a plain, normal white cloud, but I'm wondering if it's a real cloud, or if I'm imagining it, and if this is all a nightmare caused by the three-day-old pizza I ate before bed last night.

A strange growl comes from my right. Louise is stirring and does not sound very happy. She looks up with a dripping black face. I crawl to my feet and shoot up the steps onto the deck, heading inside her house. Her footsteps thump across the grass as I grab the handle of the stubborn sliding door, which hangs about two feet open. Squeezing my big butt through sideways, I give the handle a yank to close it. The door sticks. Louise is shrieking and scrambling across the deck. I give a huge jerk, and the door breaks free, sliding fast and—*WHAP!*—clamps her head hard against the metal jamb. She's held there, face halfway inside because the door's aluminum frame is sunk into the bone at her temples. She slides down the jamb to the sill, and her body slumps onto the deck behind her.

Oh Louise, I didn't want this! I'm gutted. I drop to my knees, guilt gnawing me like a rat eating my innards. I'm about to puke and then go turn myself into the cops, when something moves on her body.

An ugly black sprig sprouts out of her back, and then another. They're worming out of that spot where the creature went inside her. More slimy fingers poke out and uncurl from her and lengthen. Then a wrinkled, gooey sack squirts out and starts inflating like a water balloon full of icky black sludge.

It's returning. The creature-thing is climbing out of her.

And the weirdest thing: Louise's skin goes back to normal. All that black goop sucks back into her pores as it fills up the creature's body, leaving her coated in a clear shiny film, and me staring at the bare dead face of my good friend.

The black thing reforms and spins back into a snaky whirlwind, hissing and skittering into the house through the gap above Louise's head.

I blaze a trail for the exit, tossing over a kitchen chair behind me. The front entry stands open, so I bang through the storm screen, turn around, slam the door shut. The wood shakes when the creature thumps against the other side.

My ankle twists on my jump down the stoop. It smarts but won't slow me down. The fence gate hangs open just ten feet away, and it's the straightest shot to my house. I make it past when one of the Tisdale's windows bursts open, and the creature launches outside as though fired from a cannon. It bounces across the lawn, then rolls in a wide arc in my direction. With a boost of speed, it rockets toward me as I reach my house.

I tear open the back door and dive inside, tripping and smacking onto the floor. No time to slam the door, I just keep belly-flopping away from it. A wet thump and a slithery noise tells me the creature is now inside my home.

I steal a look back, and there it is: a ball of winding snakes ready to climb inside me.

I've got no hope but—"*Pooorrrrkchoooooop!*" I scream.

And here comes my hero, tall as a stallion, broad as a steer. Leaping clear over me, the world's best dog glides through the air like he ought to have a cape. With a snap of the jaws, he snags the creature mid-air and punches it backward onto the floor. Pouncing and snarling with that bear-trap Husky grip, Porkchop slings the thing around, slams it down and smacks it against the furniture. He must have caught it by the hind end, because he's getting the better of it.

Ready to pile on, I lunge for a poker by the fireplace, rush over and spear the thing while Porkchop has it pinned to the floor. The creature thrashes and spasms, and the sticky tentacles wrap around my ankle, but I hold it fast.

"Get him, boy! Get him!"

With a ferocious growl Porkchop snatches back his jaws. The creature's body sac tears open in a wide gash. A whole bucket's worth of bubbly black goo spills out of it and spreads in a wide pool, bleeding into the carpet of my living room.

Finally, the creature stops squirming, goes still, and deflates into a flat waxy mess.

It looks like it's finally dead.

I kneel down, rest my head on my knee, and hold my best friend tight to my body in the warmest, cuddliest hug I've ever felt. He licks my ear. I love it. So I say a little prayer, thanking the good Lord for sparing me and my dog.

When we step outside, the beating of helicopter wings draws my attention to the west, where three of the whirly-birds are flying in a circle. A ball of light streaks across the sky to the north and crashes somewhere in the vicinity of Herb and Thrillary's condo. A few suspicious plumes of smoke rise up from the hillside in the east.

The only direction that looks promising is south.

We grab a few essentials, but don't waste much time. I leave Leighton Emerson in the DVD player. Porkchop and I load up in my old Trailblazer, and we're not even to Grayson Drive before two blackened goopy maniacs step into the middle of the road, trying to block our path. One has a pickaxe. The other holds a knife in each hand. Chances are good that I know these two people, but can't recognize them.

We idle the engine about forty yards from where they're standing and think hard about what to do next.

They both rush toward us, and I can tell they aim to kill me and my favorite dog. I shift into drive and peg the accelerator like I mean to punch the pedal through the floorboard. Here we go.

Forgive me, Jesus.

I nearly puke up my coffee when the two crazies crunch beneath the tires. But I keep it between the lines and try to shut them out of my mind, because I didn't ask for any of this.

The highway is packed with cars all loaded down and headed in our same direction—away from here. Bumper to bumper, the traffic is crawling. A kid in the mini-van next to me smooshes his face against the window and waves. Looks like a lot of people are moving out and moving on.

The radio newscasters are in total hysterics, and nobody seems to know exactly what's happening.

"This is big, Porkchop. Something big's going down. Maybe we should take it as a sign that it's time for us to move on, too. What do you think?"

Porkchop looks up at me, and I swear he's got an eyebrow raised. But then he gives a friendly bark, which makes me smile, because I know that bark is dog-speak for: "I'm with you."

Slice of Heaven

The front door of the house creaked open to reveal the towering silhouette of an enormous man standing in the entryway. The dark figure stared silently for a moment and then said, "You look much more attractive in person."

Clara Littleton stood beneath his expansive shadow on the porch of his suburban home, holding a pizza. "In person?" she said, confused how the stranger had seen her otherwise.

An overhead fixture blazed to life. The man wore steel-framed spectacles, a wiry beard and a jack-o-lantern smile. His hair stood up in black tufts, and a dirty gray *Game of Thrones* T-shirt, the size of a bed sheet, draped his slouching frame.

"Saw your photo on the Slice of Heaven website." He gave her a wink.

Clara cringed. This is exactly why she hadn't wanted to participate in her boss Ned's dumb idea of posting photos of the restaurant staff on the company website; millions of creeps surfed the Internet.

"Please don't misunderstand," he added. "Your photo was lovely, but in person you're ... you're *breathtaking*." His beady eyes gleamed behind the greasy lenses.

She hated the way some men threw around flattery like a flowery smokescreen to hide their baser motives. At nineteen years old, she saw it for what it was, but offered him a "thanks" out of common courtesy. "You ordered a meat-lover's supreme, a side of cheese sticks, an apple pie and a two-liter Coke?"

The pizza balanced on her hand in a cardboard box. The side orders hung from her other in a paper sack.

"That is correct," he said.

"That'll be twenty-eight fifty."

He stretched out his thick fingers with cash folded beneath his thumb. Clara took it, avoiding the touch of his grimy nails. He smelled like a musty bathroom towel. Then she handed him the food and sorted his change. He'd given her two twenties.

"No change necessary," he said. "You keep it. My treat."

Clara peered up from her money purse. "Are you sure?"

A tip in excess of thirty percent was a rarity for pizza delivery, but she could definitely put it to use. Closing in on her second year of college, she needed cash to squirrel away for ramen noodles and diet soda.

"Absolutely," he said. "Put it in your piggy bank, Clara. You deserve it for all your hard work."

A warning sign lit red in her brain, like the check engine light ever-present on the dash of her Kia idling on the street. "So you know my face *and* my name."

"Of course," he said with a goofy smile that never wavered. "In fact, when I saw you online I asked specifically for you to deliver my order. My name is Arnold Blake."

Clara pinched her lips together and nodded. She shook his extended hand, wary of those nails. "Okay. Well, have a good night, Arnold."

Clara turned and headed to her car. Arnold Blake's leering gaze made her long for a shower, and she shuddered at the thought of how he'd conduct himself privately when staring at the online photo of her wearing the little red painter's cap emblazoned with 'Enjoy a Slice of Heaven.'

At least the creep was a good tipper.

"Bye-bye," Blake called from behind her. "See you soon, Clara."

Gross, she thought.

He was right. She soon saw him again.

***

"What's a lovely damsel like you doing at a dungeon like this?" Blake greeted through his huge smile from the doorway of his home.

The night was cold, small talk wasted time, and Clara kept strictly to business. "Delivering one large Fiery Hawaiian pizza, a side of buffalo wings, two apple pies and a Coke."

"I've been looking forward to seeing you again," he said.

"That'll be twenty-seven sixty."

"How's business at Slice of Heaven?"

Clara made sure not to sigh from exasperation. *Just do your job, keep up appearances, you need the money.* "Varies from night to night," she said. "Weekends and Thursday nights are busy. Monday nights are good during football season."

His massive head nodded up and down. "Football, yes. I guess a lot of men like their football."

"And their pizza." She hovered the flat box in front of her, prodding him to take it.

"I'm not into sports. More of a history buff, and historical fiction. I particularly enjoy medieval lore."

Clara nodded politely and bounced the pizza.

"You, for example, would make a fine maiden for one lucky suitor," he said. "May I ask, are you spoken for?"

His stalling kept her stuck on the porch, and she had little choice but to ride it out. "Um, yes," she lied. "I have a boyfriend, if that's what you mean."

"I see." For the first time, his smile faltered ever so slightly. "May I ask this lucky fellow's name?"

"Nate." Her older brother's name; he was deployed in the Air Force.

"*Nate*," Blake repeated. "Well, Nate is indeed a fortunate son."

"Anyway, that'll be twenty-seven sixty." The pizza seemed to gain weight in her hand.

"Ah, yes." He lifted it from her palm, and the cramping muscles of her forearm relaxed with cool relief. He dropped two twenties in her hand, and she gave him his bag of sides.

As she dug into her change purse, he said, "You keep the rest, fair maiden Clara. You deserve it."

"Thanks," she said. She gave him a curt salute and scampered off the porch toward her car.

"No. Thank *you*."

She could not speed away fast enough.

***

Over the next week, Arnold Blake ordered two more pizzas, each coupled with a special request that Clara deliver them to his address. She did her job dutifully, endured the man's awkward flirtations, and left with a generous tip for her troubles. Yet, with each repeat visit, his front-porch stalling tactics took longer and demanded more patience, and his small-talk grew more personally inquisitive. *How's Nate? Oh, you're taking college courses; have you decided on a major? Do you plan to marry? Would you like to have children one day?*

Although Clara needed the extra cash that Blake tipped, the very look of the man and his peculiar odor of mildew made her gag. She decided that patiently entertaining his overtures every time she delivered a pizza might send the wrong message. The easiest way to handle the problem would be to avoid it altogether.

On Friday night, she roped Brandon into taking Blake his pizza. The gangly seventeen-year-old who wore his Slice of Heaven hat backward, much to Ned's chagrin, was only too happy to have his petite blonde co-worker "owe him one."

"He's kind of a creepy guy, but he's a good tipper," Clara said. "And I'd really, really appreciate it."

"Sure, no problem," Brandon agreed with a wink.

"Thank you, thank you, thank you!" She gave him a hug and he blushed.

But when Brandon returned to the store after delivery, he gave Clara a wrinkled eyebrow and said, "Good tipper, huh? I guess I'm not his type."

"He didn't hook you up?" she said.

"Nope. Stiffed me completely."

"You're kidding."

"Negative."

"Aw, man, that sucks. I'll cut you a tip out of mine tonight. I'm so sorry he did that."

"Keep your money," Brandon said. "But you're right, the guy's a creep."

The following night she convinced a different co-worker to take the delivery. He got stiffed too.

She had Sunday night off work.

On Monday night, she caught sight of Arnold Blake following her in an old Buick as she made her deliveries.

***

"That's definitely stalker-type behavior," Brandon said when Clara told him about Blake shadowing her car. She'd noticed the vehicle on previous deliveries parked at the house where the man had his pizza delivered. It was a nineties-model green Buick with a distinctly dented hood, as though a tree limb had fallen on it.

"Maybe you should carry a pistol. At least pepper spray or something. Have you told Ned about it?"

"Yes," Clara said.

"What'd he say?"

"He took my photo off the website." She rolled her eyes. "Maybe that'll limit the number of weirdos who track me down in the future, but it doesn't help much with this one."

"You're sure he was following you? Wasn't just coincidence or something, like he was just out driving around?"

"I'm pretty sure he was tailing me. Intentionally keeping his distance. Ninety percent sure."

"Wow," Brandon said. "Probably hard for you to believe, but I myself have never had a stalker. Not sure how I'd handle it. I guess it'd depend on how she looked."

"What if *she* was six-foot-six, obese and had a beard?"

"Good point. Yeah, you have a problem."

Nothing happened on Clara's Tuesday-night delivery route. She saw no sign of the Buick, and Ned told her no one from the Blake residence had ordered a pizza that night.

***

Wednesday night was different.

"Hi Clara it is Arnold. Just ordered from Slice. Please deliver! Please please please!!"

The text buzzed on her private mobile phone at 6:22 pm.

She stared dumbly at the little glowing screen as she processed the message, and when the sense of intrusion sank in, her stomach twisted and tightened. She tugged at her collar as anger pumped her blood hot and fierce. But her skin also prickled as she mulled over the frightening lengths somebody like this—someone with zero regard for her privacy or social etiquette—might go to pursue his obsession. Her cell number was not public information. How the hell he had gotten her digits utterly mystified her. Nevertheless, she decided to play 'possum.

Do not reply, she decided. *However he'd come across the number—computer hacking, whatever—let him think he got it wrong. Let him think he's tracked down the wrong person. Don't even acknowledge receipt.*

"Your mom gave me your number." A new text vibrated the phone in her palm like a trapped insect.

Clara's breath caught in her chest.

It took a few seconds to break from her stupor. She fumbled with the phone to dial her mother's home number, hammer-tapping the keypad in a panic. The electronic ring jingled in her ear for an eternity before someone picked up.

"Hello?"

"Mom!" she accidentally shouted.

"Yes, hon. You sound out of breath. Are you okay?"

Clara realized how rapidly her heart thumped in her chest. It now gradually slowed. "Yes." She leaned back in the seat of her car with a soft, embarrassed laugh while catching her breath. "Yes, Mom, I'm fine. Just thought I'd check on you."

"Check on me? Well, I'm fine. I don't know why you'd think something might be wrong. I'm just sorting clothes for the dry cleaners. By the way, a friend of yours from the pizza store called for you. Albert or Arnie, I can't remember. I gave him your cell number. I hope that's okay."

Clara looked at her phone. She loved her mother deeply, but every once in a while felt the urge to strangle her.

***

The overhead light cast a yellow glow across the covered porch of the Blake house. Clara approached cautiously with the delivery. Aside from a single lit window upstairs, the others were darkened, yet she had the keen impression that Arnold Blake lurked somewhere within those interior shadows, watching outside with lustful anticipation. As Clara climbed the steps with the pizza and side-orders, the heavy door creaked open.

"Clara!" trumpeted Blake with obvious excitement. "I am so thrilled to lay eyes on you!"

She gave a brief nod and extended his order unceremoniously. "Hello, Arnold. Double-meat, double-cheese, bread sticks, pie and Coke. Total of twenty-seven twenty."

He wore a faded T-shirt which depicted an armored knight carrying a battle-axe and sitting astride a huge black stallion. "Some of the other drivers have been showing up here, but I don't enjoy them nearly as much as I do you."

Clara was generally adept at faking a smile and casually shooting the breeze on the job, but now found it impossible to force her lips into anything but a stiff, flat line.

"We all have a job to do. Speaking of that, I have a very busy night, so if I could just collect the cash, that'd be great. I'm really backed up on deliveries."

"You are quite a diligent employee," Blake said. "I couldn't be happier that you responded to my text."

"I didn't respond."

"But of course you did. After all, you're right here. In the flesh. Your physical presence pleases me much more than a simple electronic message, after all."

Now's your chance, Clara. Be firm but clear, and put an end to this once and for all.

"About that, Arnold. Please don't contact me directly. My phone has a private number. My mom should have never given it out. How did you track her down, anyway?"

"The White Pages. I located your sweet mother among seven other Littletons listed here in Trapper Valley."

Clara sighed. "Okay, fine. But I want you to stop contacting my phone."

The man's granite smile never faltered, even as he tilted his head, leaned forward and gazed into her eyes.

"I can't make any promises," he said. "After all, my requests to Slice of Heaven have gone unfulfilled lately, and to be frank, the refusal of your store's management to honor my requests has begun to negatively impact my experience as a paying customer. My orders are placed with the stipulation that they be delivered by you, Clara Littleton, and I am a customer who demands satisfaction. If the only way I can ensure that happens is to contact my delivery driver of choice directly—as seems to be the case—then that's the path I'll be forced to take. After all," he said through his picket fence of crooked teeth, "the customer is always right."

A chill crawled over Clara like a swarm of cold ants.

"That's twenty-seven twenty," Clara repeated, trying not to scowl blatantly at the customer, but it was getting tough.

"Your eyes are as dark as a castle moat by midnight." The man's deep voice adopted a wistful quality. "Fairest Clara, won't you lower your drawbridge and let me cross?"

"I've got a boyfriend."

Although Clara didn't think it possible, Blake's smile stretched even wider.

"No, you don't," he said. "So how about a date?"

Conscious that her jaw had fallen open, Clara snapped it shut. For a few seconds she forgot the English language, and strange garbled sounds rolled around her tongue. Finally she muttered, "No thanks, no thank you, I really don't think that would work out. And your order is twenty-seven twenty."

With his eyes boring into her like laser rays, Blake handed her two bills, a twenty and a ten, then took his food. She stirred around in her money pouch.

"Keep the change," he offered; a very modest tip, normal for anyone except Arnold Blake.

Without a word, Clara turned and walked down the steps.

"I shall count the hours until we meet again, milady," he called from behind.

Clara sped away in her Kia.

***

Driving a pizza delivery route should not involve a haunting sense of paranoia, yet Clara experienced exactly that during the next night at work. The Thursday shift was extremely busy, and the ensuing rush and chaos of schlepping pies around town helped distract her thoughts, although she kept a keen eye out for the green Buick. She thought she saw it on two different occasions, lingering several cars behind as she drove down Grayson Drive and again on Main Street. Each time she'd made a quick turn onto a side road and lost sight of the suspect vehicle.

Throughout her shift, Clara sensed that Arnold Blake hid behind every blind curve idling in wait, monitoring her whereabouts and obsessing over how to make her his possession. All the big rigs with their semi-trailers were whales on the road, each concealing a shark on the other side. She studied the shape of every headlamp in her rearview mirror, trying to identify the rectangular lights of the Buick, the left side a bit dimmer than the right side. The darker roads off the main drag, the streets with fewer houses and fewer streetlights, those were the worst, and every deep driveway, obscure offshoot or hairpin turn threatened to reveal the big man and his green machine.

Clara got wind from Brandon that Blake had placed an order with a request for her to deliver it. Seconds later a phone text vibrated in her pocket.

Blake had written a single word: "Coming?"

She paid Brandon five bucks to deliver the pizza.

At the end of the night Blake followed up with a second text to Clara's phone: "Extremely disappointed."

***

Friday night began with a text from Clara's admirer: "Fair maiden Clara, if you'll give me the chance, I'll slay all your dragons. I'll be the hero you so deserve. I'll never let you down, and my dedication to you will never falter or sway."

Good grief, Clara thought. She did not reply.

The night started smoothly for the weekend kickoff. Business was brisk, but the tips were rolling in, and the action kept her mind off the pining messages that accrued on her mobile. She'd closed it up in the glove compartment to muffle its incessant buzzing. An hour later she checked it, and her evasion had only emboldened him. She found an ongoing chain of corny romantic overtures from the contact she'd saved as "CREEP," all the notes written with forced medieval flair.

"I crave the comfort of thine embrace like some cold lost child alone in the dark."

"Every second of every day without you is like a thousand knives of fire stabbing me in the heart."

"I would part the seas for you, milady. I would swim the river Styx. Tell me the way to prove my love, and you will know the truth and understand."

He'd also left three voicemails.

When rolling down Main Street she spotted a pair of suspicious headlamps four cars behind, winking at her with the left eye. Returning from a delivery, she took a detour onto the Trapper Valley on-ramp, merged onto I-65 and took the highway one exit away to loop back through town. Patiently lingering a good fifty yards in the rear, those headlights followed her path and tailed her down the off-ramp to return in the direction they'd come.

Had to be him.

She phoned Ned.

No orders had been placed by Blake.

Because he wasn't home, naturally.

Gut instinct told her Blake had *always* been around the last few days, just over her shoulder, barely out of view. How this was possible, she did not know, and maybe her imagination fueled her unease. But she couldn't shake the feeling.

The winking vehicle moved into her lane when she exited back onto Main Street, and she wondered if her car was being tracked. The technology existed. Clara knew about Global Positioning Systems and Lojack Tracking Devices. She didn't care exactly how the science of it all worked but knew the capability was available, and a man like Arnold Blake was just the type of guy to misuse it.

If he could track her remotely, then ditching him would be pointless, but the alternative, it seemed, was *not* to try, and to accept an unacceptable situation.

A pass through the median approached on her left. With a chirp of the brakes she cut sharply past the "No U-Turn" sign, swerving to miss an old pickup that honked. She rambled back the other way.

The big Buick with the dented hood slowed too late and missed the turn. As Clara passed, she raised her middle finger from across the median, but a streetlamp glare obscured the driver. A shame, she thought. She wanted to see if that big grin of his wilted when she shot him the bird.

Clara stabbed the gas, zipped through a mixed-income development and circled back for Slice of Heaven.

"Ned, I'm pulling into the drive-thru," she told him after phoning the store. "You got an order ready to go? Anything but the Blake house."

"The drive-thru lane is for customers, Clara."

"I've got a stalker, thanks to you, and I'm not going to spend any more time than necessary at the one place he would expect me to be. With that in mind, maybe you can just slide the next order out the window to me."

"Has this guy actually threatened you?"

This was the third time Ned had asked her the same question over the last few days.

"Not yet, Ned."

After a silent pause, he said, "Clara, are you sure you're not—"

"Have the pizza ready, Ned!" She hung up.

She rolled up next to the sliding window of the restaurant. Brandon, wearing a big smile, handed her a pizza into the car, stacked with an order of breadsticks. "I think you hurt Ned's feelings when you yelled at him," he whispered. "He's been whining about it to everyone in here."

Clara rolled her eyes. "Good grief."

"You're the only one who can get away with that."

"I'm special, I guess." She gave him a wave and rolled on down the road.

As expected, the winking vehicle soon made a reappearance in the distance behind her. Her pulse quickened and she instinctively gave the car more gas.

As Clara snaked her way toward the delivery address, she would lose sight of the car occasionally, but then see it round a turn, those white eyes emerging from the blackness in her rearview. Then she'd lose them again.

The possibility that Arnold Blake might pose a real physical danger was an idea that began to gnaw at her with sharp teeth. But, admittedly, Ned had a point; Blake had never made a threat. She had nothing but his love notes to make a case against him. Would the cops take her seriously if she filed a complaint?

Either way, she only had a couple weeks left to stick it out. Clara had a mere fifteen days left at the Slice of Heaven to save up some desperately needed money before fall semester began. Before she moved back to college, saw her friends again, returned to her medical studies and got her life back on track. She would not allow Arnold Blake to stand in the way of those plans.

The delivery address took her to a secluded cul-de-sac. Her parking spot of choice—the curb—was occupied with other vehicles, so she pulled across the street. As she cut the engine and unclicked her seatbelt, she heard the low bass thump of a stereo. She gathered the order and stepped out of the car as pulsing synth music pounded out a driving beat from the house. Sounded like a party.

She gazed up the street and waited, expecting the winking eyes of the Buick to crest the hilltop. The road led down into a dead-end with a small circle wide enough to turn around. Only one way in and one way out. The street had branched off a new subdivision. Three lots surrounded the circle; the party house, an empty new home with a "for sale" sign in the yard, and a foundation under construction. When Clara saw no sign of Arnold Blake she went to the house and knocked.

The bass thumped behind the door. *Oomf, oomf, oomf*

The door opened to a bright interior, and the music blared out like a burst dam.

"Hey there!" greeted a young man who bobbed his head to the rhythm. He wore a tank top and had his brown hair combed back with product. "How you doing?"

"Got your pizza!" Clara shouted over the din of the stereo.

"Oh, right!" said another boy who appeared over the shoulder of the first, bare-chested, taller and slimmer with feathery blond hair. "I ordered that. I'm Chance," he said and wiped his nose. He, too, moved in sync with the music.

Oomf, oomf, oomf

"Hey, come on in," the first boy said, slipping his arm around Clara and sweeping her into the house before she could stop him. "My name's Pete. Hey, didn't you go to Trapper Valley High?"

Entering a customer's house was a firm rule Clara knew never to break.

"I graduated last year," she replied to Pete, just to remain polite.

Near the TV another boy, with an athletic build, black hair and bronze skin, bounced on the balls of his feet while pumping his fists like he was preparing for a cardio workout. He gave a wave and a nodding smile.

The house was built with a open floor plan, but messy, with liquor bottles cluttering the coffee table and beer cans piled in the kitchen sink. A bong stood next to an ashtray and a fat bag of grass. On the countertop lay a mirror, a razor, and a box of half-eaten pizza.

Oomf, oomf, oomf

"Yeah, I think I remember you," Chance said from behind her.

She turned as Chance closed the front door. His fingers slid down to the deadbolt, pinched the knob, and turned it to the lock position.

The hairs on Clara's neck stood up.

"Damn, you're fine," said the bronze athlete across the room. "What's your name, chica?"

She swallowed thickly. "Clara." It took concerted effort to keep her voice steady. "And the total comes to twenty-two fifty."

"Yeah, that's cool," Pete said and rubbed his nose. His mouth had a tic as though his lip bothered him. "We'll pay in a minute. No rush, baby. We ain't rushin' tonight, we're partyin'." Pete lifted a bottle of tequila from the table, tilted it upside-down and took a generous gulp. He squinted, shook his head and howled at the ceiling.

"Hell yeah, we are," Chance said.

"You want to party with us, girl?" the nameless boy called at her. He bounced over to the kitchen counter, throwing little jabs in the air. He leaned over and snorted something off the mirror.

"I just need to collect the money and go," Clara said. "I'm on duty. Busy night."

"Aw, man. No way. You need to stay," Chance said.

With his hand against her lower back, he tried to press her further into the room. She stiffened with resistance. Her instinct demanded she swat him away, but both hands carried the order. She spun away from him. When she bent to set the pizza down on the coffee table, groping fingers caressed her bottom. She spun around and spat, "Stop it!"

Both Pete and Chance only grinned.

"Are you going to pay for this or what?" She held their gaze defiantly, but inside she felt the walls closing in.

"Look, don't get excited," Chance said, stepping nearer, at least a head taller and looking down his long nose. "We just want to have a little fun."

He cuffed her wrists with his hands and pulled her close.

She shoved him back. "Get the hell off me!"

Oomf, oomf, oomf

"Whoa, wait a minute!" Pete said. The smile melted and his expression hardened. "There's no need to have a bitchy attitude. We're just having a good time is all."

"I'm not here for a good time. If you're not paying I'm leaving." Clara went for the door.

A hand grabbed her belt and pulled her backward. This time she whirled around and karate-chopped Pete's arm from its grip. "Leave me alone!"

"Bitch!" Pete lunged, grabbed her shirt collar and snatched her face into his. "You don't wanna piss me off!"

She shoved him off, and when he came back, she fired a fist forward. *Bingo!* The punch struck dead center of his nose. The fleshy tip pushed between her knuckles with a satisfying pop, and he staggered backward, holding his face.

"Aggghhh! You're gonna pay for that!"

Chance pulled her to the floor from behind. The nameless guy ran over and clutched her ankles, pulling her legs straight to stifle her kicking. So fast, their hands were everywhere.

"Get off me!"

Oomf, oomf, oomf

"Shut up, bitch!" Pete leapt astride her and jammed his forearm over her mouth. "Just shut the fuck up!"

Clara bit down hard, and he yelled.

Pete jerked up his arm, balled a fist and hammered it down. Clara turned and took the blow to the cheekbone. Hot nails shot through her face muscles. Fireworks exploded in her eyes. The prodding pressure of groping fingers pushed into her crotch, and she squirmed. The sound of ripping fabric and popping buttons came from her blouse—and then a familiar electronic chirp.

While punching and thrashing, Clara spotted her phone on the floor from the corner of her eye. It must have fallen out in the melee. The thing buzzed aglow, chirping an incoming call. The screen illuminated the contact name: CREEP.

Clara darted her head up and chomped Pete's arm. He rolled off, and in that instant she crunched her legs and kicked the bronze boy. Thrashing to the side, she spun onto her stomach, tore free from Chance and made a reaching dive for the phone. Her fingertip tapped the screen, which went green with connection.

"Arnold!" she shrieked at the top of her lungs. "Arnold, please help me!"

With a depressing crunch, Chance's high-top Nike stomped the phone beneath it. The shattered screen went black. He gave her a hard stare and a humorless grin.

The other hands retook their grip, rubbing and digging at her clothes. She bucked and twisted, clawed and snapped her teeth. The boys, smelling of sweat and liquor, grunted and licked their lips.

"Get off me!" Clara demanded over and over.

"Keep quiet and you won't get hurt!" Pete growled as he tore off his shirt and crammed it into her mouth.

Over the chaos of the music and shouts, a knock came from the door.

"You hear that?" said no-name.

"What?" Pete said as he tore open Clara's buttoned shirt to reveal her bra. Chance held her hands behind her head.

Three heavy thuds came from the door.

"*That!*" the boy said.

"Who the fuck is that?" Chance said to the others.

The bronze-skinned boy shot over to the entry. Through the door he shouted, "Who is it?"

Oomf, oomf, oomf

Clara's writhing fit gained new strength. She strained to wiggle free, so desperate for her muffled screams to be heard by whoever was knocking.

The boy pressed his ear to the door to hear the response. Then he threw the latch and opened the slab a crack, just to peek outside and ask the unwanted visitor, "Who the fuck are—"

Clara froze as a long shaft of steel burst from the back of no-name's white shirt. A dark circle of red formed around the exit point. For a long second, he stood there statuesque except for the trembling fingers of his right hand. The other two boys were too busy fumbling with Clara to notice, but she couldn't tear her eyes away.

No-name flew backward into the room from a fierce boot to the gut. He spun and fell, the sword clanging against a metal coatrack at his side. His face hit the hardwood with a whap. A large black hilt protruded from his chest, and his mouth made quiet fishlike movements while gasping for air.

Pete's raunchy sneer wilted when he saw the beast explode through the doorway, as big as an ox and bearing a huge metal shield crested with a coat of arms.

"*Unhand the girl!*" boomed the Viking demand of Arnold Blake, as he advanced on the two pinning Clara to the floor.

"What the hell!" Chance cursed. He released Clara, rose into a three-point stance and lunged into a spear-like tackle at the intruder. But Blake had the shield for defense—and something at his hip. The big man lifted it high as Chance shot forward. From a club-like handle hung a heavy chain with a spiked metal ball, and Blake slung it in an arc. Chance slapped to the floor when the ball punched down between his shoulder blades.

"*holy shit, oh my god...*" Pete muttered, recoiling from Clara who spat out the shirt and rolled away from him.

Arnold Blake spun the mace overhead with fire in his eyes, and that pumpkin grin spread impossibly wide through his wiry black beard. *Whoosh-whoosh*—he brought it down onto the back of Chance's skull with a muddy smack. Chance stopped moving.

Pete swiped a beer bottle from the coffee table. He gripped it by the neck and smashed its bottom on the ledge.

It took two tugs for Blake to dislodge the weapon from Chance's head, the spikes having stuck in the bone.

"Die, you fucker!" Pete snarled as he thrust the jagged glass at Blake's throat.

The big man swung the mace into Pete's shoulder, smashing it out of shape and slamming him into the wall.

Again, that spiked ball circled Blake's head like a hungry buzzard. Pete backed into the corner, dropped to his knees, shielded his face and whimpered. Arnold Blake rained hell down upon him. First he broke the boy's arms. Then, with damp, crunching blows, the spikes ripped Pete's skull wide open and showered everything with blood. Blake kept right on swinging and rending him to mush. At last, Pete's splattered body toppled over with an unrecognizable mound dangling from the shoulders.

Clara found herself curled into a ball on the floor and surrounded by corpses. Her every nerve ending had a dull sensation like a burnt fuse. She could not shut her eyes. She could not blink. She could barely breathe.

Arnold Blake stood over Pete's carcass still holding the medieval-style weapon loosely, but triumphantly, at his side. Judging from his heaving form, he too was catching his breath. Blake dropped the mace and the shield where he stood. He turned and approached Clara, who hugged herself and shook all over.

A shard of glass protruded from a cut in his neck that bled in a steady stream. It spread in a large dark patch across his faded black T-shirt, which depicted a scythe-wielding reaper riding a demonic winged serpent. Blake's glasses were speckled with red, and he removed them, folded them, and hung them from his collar. He wiped off his face and cleaned his hands on his jeans. Then he stumbled and caught himself on the wall. With a cough, he knelt over Clara on a single knee, his hulking frame listing back and forth, and he stretched out his palm.

"Oh, fairest Clara, I am so relieved to see you unharmed." His voice sounded raspy and weak. "I am so glad you're now safe. I thank the gods I was able to respond to your call in time." He curled a crooked smile that gleamed as big as she'd ever seen it.

Clara studied his palm like it was a foreign object. A million thoughts and fears raced through her mind.

"This ugly mess is all behind us now," he said. "Now we can return to happier times. So … about that date?"

Clara, shaken to the core by the terror and violence, and numb inside and out, could not effectively respond to the offer. Her world was still spinning, and all she wanted was her mother. She could never bring herself to say "yes" to Blake's request for a date. Yet, at the moment she could not seem to form the word "no."

She looked him in the eyes and had a single hazy thought from somewhere deep down in her soul: *Good grief…*

Slowly, she reached to take his hand. But Arnold Blake fell over dead.

Cookies

Emmy Beemer tiptoed through the deep shadows of the dark kitchen holding her footstool. She quietly climbed its two little steps and stretched to open the cabinet door. The hinge squeaked, and she froze, praying the noise had not stirred her stepfather sleeping down the hallway. After a moment, she slid a paper plate from the shelf and reached for the cookie jar on the counter. Its steel lid gave an airy ping as it pulled free, and Emmy winced. She pulled out three chocolate chip cookies, added them to the platter, and then grabbed a banana from the nearby fruit bowl.

Emmy liked bananas, so maybe the thing in the trees would too. It definitely liked cookies. But she'd been taught that a diet consisting only of cookies was not a healthy one.

Creeping through the kitchen with the plate held flat, Emmy made her way to the back door of the house. Slowly and steadily, she pinched the deadbolt latch between her fingers. This was always the worst part. With teeth clenched tight, she gave a twist. The deadbolt slid back with a *thunk!* that echoed throughout the room.

Emmy held her breath and listened. Her heart thumped in her ears. The refrigerator hummed from the kitchen. But that was all she heard—not the heavy footsteps of a grown man disturbed from his sleep.

She pulled on the heavy door, which popped and creaked. She drew it halfway open, just enough room to slip past and push open the screen door.

A cool breeze rushed into the house and ruffled her curly brown hair. Emmy placed the plate on the deck, just outside, then looked up to an overcast sky. Few stars shined above, and the moon looked fuzzy. She found it difficult to make out the inky branches of the skeletal trees that loomed above her back yard. That's where the thing lived, somewhere up there, crawling around, leaping from limb to limb, and watching. She wouldn't see it. Not tonight. The light had to be just right, and she had a hunch that when the thing did not want to be seen, no one would see it.

She got her first glimpse of it two weeks ago from the deck of her house. It had made a noise which caught her attention. She'd sat alone on the steps that clear autumn night, blowing bubbles through a small plastic ring, when a low, chattering sound, almost a buzz, came from the trees. At the time, a few dead leaves still clung to the branches, and Emmy peered up to see an odd shape perched among them on a thick limb far overhead. It moved with quick, jerky motions and had long, slender limbs—more than four—like some strange, gangly insect that might hide in your slipper and crunch beneath your bare foot. But this thing was much bigger than any bug she'd ever seen.

Its head, if that's what it was, shook from side-to-side and gave a string of soft chirps, which sounded in no way dangerous to Emmy. In fact, it sounded cute and put her at ease. She took the noise as a greeting.

"Hello," Emmy had answered the thing in the trees.

A twinkle in its eyes told her she'd made a new friend. Then the shadow's head wiggled and chirped again, and the creature leapt up to the higher branches, climbing the tree with cat-like speed and grace. It disappeared as it shot over to a neighboring tall pine.

Since then, she had been leaving it snacks. And it had been eating what she fed it—at least some of the food. Always the cookies. And she caught glimpses of the creature only once in a while. On the lucky nights.

Emmy closed the doors. She twisted the deadbolt, which clicked with a smaller noise than when unlocking it, and tiptoed back to her room.

***

Cold air swept over Emmy. She opened her eyes to the raging voice of her stepfather as he ripped away the bedsheets that covered her.

"What have I told you!" he shouted. "Time and time again, I told you! No sweets in the middle of the night. No *sweets!*"

He hit the light switch, and Emmy squinted from the painful glare.

"But whad'ya know! The first thing I find when I wake up is the damn cookie jar left open in the kitchen," he said. "Now all the cookies have gone soft and shitty. That's why you're supposed to seal 'em up and not leave 'em open!"

Emmy stuttered and grunted.

"What's the problem, Dale?" asked her mom in a groggy voice from somewhere down the hallway.

"Nothing I can't handle!" Dale shouted to her over his shoulder. He turned back to Emmy and frowned through the grainy beard that circled his mouth, staring down at her with cold, gray eyes. "If I'd wanted the cookies to be all soft and shitty, then I'd have bought the soft and shitty kind at the grocery store. As far as I'm concerned, these are ruined. You ruined 'em 'cause you disobeyed. I guess I just wasted money on this brand-new pack of cookies I bought yesterday. Which is just par for the course around here, since I'm the only one who *brings in* any money! No wonder I'm the only one with any goddamn appreciation for it!"

"I told you," called Emmy's mother from the other end of the house. "I'm looking for a job."

He turned toward the hallway and roared, "Shut up, Maureen!"

Emmy rubbed her eyes and realized Dale was holding the open cookie jar. He raised it in front of him with both hands and flipped it upside down. All the remaining cookies tumbled out and spilled all over her bedroom floor.

"Clean those up and get ready for school."

***

As Emmy walked up to her porch from the bus stop after school, Dale's raised voice boomed out of the walls. The thump of stomping feet rumbled from one end of the house to the other. He shouted and cursed about his job, calling his boss a son-of-a-this and a mother-that. Emmy decided not to open the door. She turned around and sat down on the front stoop.

Beneath her, on the cracked concrete walkway, a single black ant carried a quarter-sized piece of potato chip that dwarfed the little critter. Emmy wondered if the ant was a cousin to the thing in the trees. She bent closer and studied its fierce determination.

"I wish I was as strong as you," she whispered.

The ant ignored her.

Big things almost always took advantage of little things, except the ant was different. Not like her. She had to put up with Dale because he was stronger. She was just like her friends who rode the school bus. Red-headed Phillip had a mean mother who would sometimes lock him in the closet. Her friend Bethany, whose Mom would give her the most beautiful braids, also had a father who would rub her in uncomfortable ways and make her sit on his lap funny. Emmy, Red-headed Phillip and Bethany had to put up with such things because they were weaker than the people who did it to them, and they were afraid to do anything about it.

From somewhere inside the house came another voice—her mother's. Emmy had hoped that Dale was yelling into his phone. Her mother was not always home when she arrived from school, but it appeared her mom was today, which put her right in Dale's warpath.

Emmy left the ant and went into the house. She'd learned that Dale was less likely to strike her mother when she was around to witness the abuse.

Dale continued his tirade in the master bedroom, so she shouted, "Mom, I'm home!" then headed into the kitchen. Two grocery bags sat on the counter, still full. Dale must have ambushed her mom with news of his bad day before the groceries could be put away. Emmy lifted her footstool from its place in the corner and carried it to the counter. She climbed up to unload the bags and sort things out.

Among the items, Emmy found a new package of cookies, the shortbread kind with fudge stripes. For the first time that day, she smiled.

***

Dale eventually hollered his throat hoarse and left to get beer with a slam of the front door. Emmy walked to the other end of the house to check on her mother. Sobbing came from the bathroom. Emmy approached the fist-sized hole that Dale had punched through the door a month ago. Instead of fixing the damage, he had only thumbtacked a hand towel over the hole to give the bathroom back its privacy.

The jagged edges of the wood formed the open jaws of a hungry mouth. Emmy leaned into the hole. "Mom, are you okay?"

A hiccup and a sniff were her only answers.

"Mom, are you hurt?"

"I'm okay, hon. Don't worry about me. I'll be fine."

Her mother's soft cries passed right through the thin linen, and Emmy took in every hushed sound.

"I'll be right back," she said.

Standing atop her stepstool, Emmy pulled a tray of ice cubes from the freezer. She walked to the sink, held it over the basin, and twisted the plastic tray. With a sharp crackle, the ice broke loose of the little square cups. She dropped three cubes into a plastic zip-lock baggie and sealed it up tight.

Emmy moved the stepstool further down the counter to reach the paper towels. She unspooled two, wrapped them around the plastic to pad the compress, and returned to the bathroom.

"Here you go," Emmy said to her mom through the door. Ice in hand, Emmy pushed past the towel curtain and reached through the hole. After a sniffle, her mom came over and took the cool bundle. She then returned to her spot on the toilet lid, where she always cried alone.

"Thanks, hon."

"You're welcome."

Mom often needed ice after Dale had been yelling.

***

The back door parted with a pop and a creak. Emmy pushed open the screen door, and the familiar gust of chilly air blew through the cotton fabric of her t-shirt. Twinkling stars and a full moon lit the midnight sky with a purple glow that outlined the scraggly trees overhead. She stepped onto the deck with a plate of cookies in hand, and eased the door closed behind her.

Almost barren of leaves, the wide web of overlapping branches bent and split and criss-crossed to form a busy patchwork, like the sky had shattered and the broken shards had yet to fall to earth.

High above her, and perched near the trunk of a tall oak, Emmy made out a shape. When it moved its spindly limbs, all jerky and weird, she knew she'd found the creature.

"Hi," she greeted through a cupped whisper, hoping with her biggest wish that it would greet her back, that it would somehow acknowledge her presence. "I brought you more cookies. And an apple tonight."

The shadow in the tree tilted its head and wiggled its body.

"Apples are good," she said. The thing hadn't eaten the banana, but Emmy hadn't thought to peel it. She'd found last night's plate with only crumbs of the cookies but the full banana, with small gnaw marks on the tough stem of its peel. The creature hadn't made it to the sweetness of the soft fruit inside. The thin peel of an apple would be easier to get past.

With the squeal of a hinge, the house door flew open. A loud bang, and the storm screen swung outward. Bright yellow light poured onto the deck behind the dark shape of Dale Roberts, who rubbed his eyes while muttering words that Emmy was not allowed to say.

"You woke me up, ya little dumbass," Dale said. "Goddammit. And looky here. Caught red-handed. Disobeyin' me, just like we talked about."

Dale seemed to grow in size while Emmy shrank. She stared up at his dark, towering shape, and then dropped her eyes to the plate of cookies. She tried to swallow but her mouth went dry as dust.

Dale batted the plate out of her hand. The apple bounced across the deck and rolled off the edge to the ground below. The cookies lay scattered everywhere. Emmy dropped to her knees and snatched them up, collecting three in the hem of her t-shirt. Dale lifted his knee and stomped the other cookies into powder with snarling curses.

"I told you no sweets at *midnight*!" he shouted. "No friggin' *sweets*!"

The wood shook beneath Emmy. She backed away and clutched her shirt together.

"What is it about the word 'no' you don't understand!"

Her eyes clouded, and hot tears rolled down her face. Part of her so badly wanted Mom, but another part didn't.

"I'm sorry," Emmy said. "Please don't be mad! I'm so sorry!"

"You're always sorry! You and your mom both, the sorriest people I ever met!"

Maybe Mom would hear and come anyway. Or, maybe Mom had taken a pill and wouldn't wake up.

"I've had it with you two," Dale said. "I really have." His nostrils flared, and his whole body heaved with his bull-like breaths.

"Don't hurt me," Emmy said. "Please, Dale."

"Why not?" he said. "'Cause it don't seem to me that anything else is gettin' through to you. I've told you time and time again. But you keep right on disobeyin'."

He leaned closer, just inches from Emmy's face. His body heat clouded around her.

"Maybe," he continued with his breath stinking of beer and tuna, "maybe I oughtta blister your little bottom."

Emmy backed into the corner where the deck railing met the house wall—trapped with nowhere to run. The tears were beyond her control. She could barely breathe.

"Maybe," Dale said, "I oughtta bend you over and jerk down those panties. Take off my belt and show you how my daddy used to punish me."

He lifted his hands, working his fingers eagerly. He was coming for her, plain as day, and he was so huge. Emmy clutched her ears and sank down into a ball.

He grabbed her by the shoulders.

But a heavy thump on the deck brought him to a stop. He turned his head slightly and squinted, listening to a reedy, chirping noise behind him. He released Emmy and spun around.

"What the hell?!" Dale lurched back, nearly falling onto her.

The thing from the trees stood upright on the deck atop four hind legs. Maybe five feet tall, it had a segmented body with a shiny underside. Shell-like armor covered its skinny legs and torso, and its upper limbs floated in front of it like angry, jointed snakes. Two long, thin antennae extended above two huge eyes that looked like black tomatoes, their surface shimmering with countless gleaming lenses. And two pincer-like jaws twitched at its mouth as it made the chirping noise.

"He's my friend," Emmy said.

Her friend took a lurch forward, stretched its head at Dale and gave a furious hiss.

"Like hell!" Dale snatched a nearby broom from where it leaned against the house. He swung it in a wide homerun arc that clobbered Emmy's friend. With a crunch, the creature slammed into the house siding from the blunt force of the thick wooden handle.

"Leave him alone!" Emmy screamed.

Dale drew back and flipped the broom. He struck again with the handle end, thwacking it into the thing's limbs, crashing it back into the wall.

Emmy leapt onto Dale's back and clawed at him. He shook her off, lifted a foot and kicked her square in the chest with his slipper. The blow shot her backward, like she'd been jerked with a rope. Her bottom pounded onto the deck, sending a sharp jolt through her.

Back on the creature, Dale beat it mercilessly where it had fallen. Its limbs thrashed and squirmed. Dale cussed and snarled as he caned the thing. The creature's angry hiss became a frightened moan. Then Dale lifted the broom handle, brought it down like a spear and skewered the creature.

"*Nooo!*" Emmy wailed, and the creature's moan deflated to a weak, voiceless rattle.

"This ain't no sort of friend," Dale muttered, catching his breath. "Some freak of nature! Mutant grasshopper or some shit."

She threw her hands to her mouth as the creature went silent and motionless. The twinkle in its eyes went dim like a cooling ember.

Something fragile inside Emmy cracked apart and collapsed to pieces.

"You ruin *everything!*"

Dale gave a hoarse laugh. "Whatever it was, now it's *dead.*" And with that, he gave a final stomp to the creature's mid-section — and he howled as soon as he did.

Dale jumped up and down on one foot.

"Ow! Shit! What the hell!" He bounced over the thing's body while groping his other leg. The tail of the creature clung to his calf as if somehow attached. "Goddamn thing stung me!"

With the husk of the creature tangled beneath, Dale shook his leg and kicked outward, but it was still stuck against him. Finally, he stamped his foot down on the thing's midsection, gripped the tail like a beer can, then twisted and pulled. The tail tore away from a long, spiny thorn that remained snared in his calf. Where the hard shell snapped off, an oozing slime leaked from the squirming organ which wiggled on the end of the stinger. Dale grunted and fell on his butt. His eyelids peeled back from the whites.

"What the hell is stuck on me?!"

Emmy wondered the exact same thing, as the wriggling tail shortened. The head of the stinger burrowed into Dale's flesh as he whimpered and clutched his leg. It swelled his flesh as it dug beneath the skin, raising a quivering lump beneath the fabric of his ratty sweatpants. He swatted at it in a panic. The lump traveled up the knee, and Dale screamed. It appeared further up his thigh, and he rose to his feet and chased it with clutching, frantic hands.

"Stop it! Stop it! *Stop it!*" he cried in a high, shaky pitch.

Emmy followed Dale's frenetic slapping toward the crotch of his pants. She'd never heard such a racket from a grown man. Twice, he socked himself hard in the crotch. He drove a fist into his gut. As the lump climbed higher, pulsing and growing, Dale used his muscular arms to slug himself in the ribs and beat himself about the chest. The blows were brutal, and his face twisted with each wallop to his body.

The swelling reached his neck, and Dale stopped breathing. He clutched at his collar. He dropped to his knees as snot ran from his nose and sweat rolled down his cheeks. His throat expanded like a balloon, stretching to twice its size. Dale's once-white eyes went cherry-red and rolled backward. His whole head shook and his mouth stretched open. A quivering black mound surged outward with a glut of thick mucus, ripping Dale's lower jaw from its hinge. His cheeks split open as a fat, veiny blob slithered out of his throat, bringing with it a short tail that wagged behind. It plopped down onto the deck.

Emmy had never seen such a monstrous tadpole.

Dale toppled over next to it, and blood spilled from his face. His eyes went glassy. He didn't move.

The tadpole-thing stopped shuddering. Emmy watched and waited. She knelt closer, inching toward it without a breath. The dark skin suddenly rippled and then peeled from around the top like a budding flower. Inside, six gnarled gray clumps rolled out onto the deck and began to uncurl. Slowly, each revealed several slender, insectoid appendages.

A gasp escaped her. The six little creatures took form and looked around, scuttling in circles. They explored one another, trading close looks and curious sniffs. One gave a prod to Dale's body, then immediately lost interest and returned to its brethren. The little pack huddled together and appeared to devise a plan. Then they all scurried over to one of the discarded cookies laying on the deck. The shortbread kind with fudge stripes. They devoured it enthusiastically, and Emmy clasped her hands with joy.

They moved a few feet over and shared another cookie.

Quickly, Emmy shot into the house, ran to a hall closet and returned with a shoebox. She collected the creatures into it—along with another cookie—and took them inside. She hid them under her bed before waking her mother to tell her that something terrible had happened to Dale.

***

Emmy stayed home from school the following week, having been excused to mourn a parent. "*Step*-parent," she would always add.

She didn't do much mourning, though. Neither did Mom, although her mother made sure to fluster and pout when adults were present. The week they spent together was magical; they picnicked, flew kites in the park, and danced in the sunshine. They stayed up late, painted each other's nails, ate ice cream and shared secrets.

But Emmy didn't tell all her secrets. She returned to school the following Monday and carried two gifts in her backpack for her friends on the bus ride home. She'd been feeding the babies, and they'd grown to the size of grapefruits.

After school, she took the bus seat ahead of Red-headed Phillip and Bethany with the braids. She pulled out two folded paper lunch sacks, leaned over the backrest and handed one to each of them.

"Here, I brought you presents."

They both smiled and took the sacks, unfurling the tops. They peered inside, and Phillip's face brightened. Bethany looked confused.

"Thanks," Phillip said. "But what are they?"

Emmy smiled. "They're pets."

"Oh, wow," Bethany said. "Neat pets!"

"Be nice and feed them, and they'll grow a lot bigger," Emmy said. "And maybe one day, they'll protect you when you need it."

Phillip and Bethany looked at each other, and then back to Emmy.

She winked. "They prefer cookies."

Gas Pedal

The first stoplight outside our subdivision must be the longest fucking traffic signal in three counties. It never fails to turn red when it sees me. Two cars are stopped ahead of me, both idiots blabbing into their phones. No other lane to pass. The light turns green, but both cars just sit there. Neither driver is paying attention, both jawing into their mobiles without a care in the world and evidently no place to be.

I pound the horn, demanding both vehicles blow to pieces in a fiery explosion. God, I wish these assholes could hear me cursing them.

The first car pulls through the intersection, but the second driver, a tough guy, eyeballs me in his rearview mirror and just sits there. He's taunting me by blocking the lane. The bass of his speakers is rattling my car. I promise him through the windshield that I will smash out his teeth with the pipe wrench laying on the floorboard if he doesn't move his vehicle. Finally, it rolls forward. He takes a left. I swerve past and spit at his bumper.

If I don't make it across town in ten minutes, then my whole plan falls apart. So, it'd be a good idea for all pedestrians to evacuate the route between me and where I'm going. I am an unstoppable force. I'm a laser-guided cruise missile.

I'd been delivering Mom's lunch to the nursing home, just like every morning, when my runaway life suddenly picked up significant downhill speed. My stupid bitch of a wife sent me an errant text message meant for that cocksucker, Gary Davidson. *"Meet you in 10 at the Continental, Sexy!"* It seems she's headed for an afternoon screw at the high-rise hotel over on Highway 11.

Mom had warned me about her, and I should have listened. Deep down in my gut I've known for a while what's been going on. And now I'm going to catch them in the act. When you're cheating on your husband, you should pay close attention who you're sending your dirty notes to.

I drive faster. Some old crone with a giant purse is crossing the street. She'd better run. She does and shouts something as I whiz by her. Old ladies run like chickens.

If I hit the main drag moving like I am, I'll have a cop on my tail in no time. So, I stay on the side streets, ignoring the stop signs. The hammer's to the floor, and this rundown Chevy is really motoring. But it's a hilly roadway; I lose speed at every dip and bottom-out with a heavy bang. The suspension is screeching, and it feels like I might lose a wheel. But screw the car. It's only got to make it a few more miles, then I won't need it anymore.

That evil harpy. She was happy as a pig in slop when there was money in the bank, when I took a position I didn't want at her father's bigshot brokerage firm. I hated the job, but it provided the uppity lifestyle she wanted. How was I to know her dad was a crook, had embezzled millions, and we'd lose everything? Get blacklisted. Every move I ever made had been done for her, all to make her happy.

The road broadens into a four-lane. Each driver I weave past blares their horn and flips me off, but they can all go straight to hell. Now back to a two-lane. Some old fart who can barely see over his steering column is clogging my path. He doesn't deserve to be on the road. I jam my front end next to his and stomp the gas. I wedge him over. *Boom!* His green land-barge slams into a parked car or three.

I see the hotel's sign coming up, overlooking all the expensive vehicles in the lot. The fancy accommodations don't impress me. It still feels like my wife's been giving it up in a pay-by-the-hour ass shack, like some truck-stop whore.

I pull across the street and idle, looking over the place. I spot her Mercedes. Holy shit, there's Gary Davidson getting out of his new BMW and walking over to meet my wife. She and Gary embrace in the middle of the lot and greet with a kiss. How sweet.

I'd planned on caving in his skull with the wrench, but I'm not married to that idea. I grab my phone and type a reply to her errant message—"Be there in just a sec!"—and hit send. Then I buckle up.

Modern technology is a marvel. She gets the text almost instantly, and I've already started accelerating. She checks her phone and furrows her brow. Confused, dear?

I murder the gas pedal. Tires squeal on the pavement. She and Gary are now gawking at my car. I'm laughing like hell as they grow very large very fast. He shoves her out the way. I cream him, and his face shatters on my windshield. The car bucks, but I keep the gas throttled and head straight for the block wall at the edge of the lot. This is going to hurt.

When we crash I feel like I'm plunged underwater.

But that doesn't last long.

I'm back in the car. Vision's blurry, but Gary has met his maker. The impact pinched his body between the crumpled hood and the wall, and a gob of pink goo has squirted from his mouth like he was a human tube of toothpaste. I hit the wipers.

I hear precious wifey screaming. I grab the wrench from the floorboard and kick open the crunched car door. When she sees me, I can tell from her expression that she's struggling with a number of regrets. Sirens are wailing a few blocks away. Here comes the cavalry. But I only need a few more minutes, a little private time up close, to make sure I leave her with a face that no man will ever want to kiss again.

***

"You're nobody..."

Now, I'm in Gary's Beamer. Nice ride, but it's hard to focus on that because I'm so worked up over my wife and her big mouth. A total bitch until the bitter end, that one.

"You're nobody, you bastard!" she told me, bawling about her dead lover. "You never amounted to shit! You're sick, and you're nobody!"

She always had to get the last word in edgewise. Congratulations, dear.

I showed her that I'm not a man of words, I'm a man of action. I introduced her to the pipe wrench. Three or four times. That shut her up; her lips now a mass of raw hamburger. She used to be beautiful.

"I'm nobody?" I said. "After all I've done for you? You toss me to the side as soon as times get tough ... You stab me in the back, then tell me I'm *nobody?*"

The cop sirens blared behind me. My muscles tightened, and I figured my time was up. But as I turned around, the trio of cruisers, lights flashing like fireworks, blazed right past the hotel parking lot and shot down the street. Stupid assholes.

My wife gave a whimper, and I smiled like a blue-ribbon winner.

"No, Dearest, you'll soon see that I'm *somebody!*" I told her. "In fact, you made me the man that I've become. And I'm going to let you live to regret it."

I left her there, mangled and bleeding, and hit the road.

***

You're nobody… Her voice echoes in my head. Something about those words has finally fried my last nerve.

I feel the cogs in my brain binding and stripping.

Nobody? Wrong. Maybe my life's in a tailspin, but I'll show you that I'm *somebody*.

I'm going out with a bang.

And I'll bet a fine bottle of bourbon that my name will be all over the local news within hours.

Yeah. That's the ticket.

She and everyone else will hear the last gory detail. Publicity like I've got in mind turns a *nobody* into a *somebody* in no time.

And if you really put the hammer down, if the needle hits the red line and you keep right on truckin', then you might even make the national news. That's when you really become *somebody*.

Let me show you.

At my apartment, no cops are in sight. I give myself two minutes tops, grab the shotgun and a box of shells.

Back on the road, a little calmer, I'm cruising down Highway 78. Things are chill. A BMW is a finely tuned piece of machinery, and the ride is smooth like I'm gliding on a boulevard of warm butter. I turn on the radio and learn that Gary Davidson was a fan of soul music. Al Green is singing softly about how he's still in love with me, which cools me down like a damp towel. With the windows open, the breeze feels nice.

I pass a school bus. Trapper Valley Elementary is stenciled on the side. Must be a field trip. The kids stretch weird faces and laugh at me through the windows. Ahead of the bus is an antique Cadillac convertible with an older couple, both with white hair. The top is down.

The streetlight ahead turns red. I stop at the intersection alongside the convertible. The man driving has a cigarette in his mouth. He takes it out, leans over and kisses his wife on the cheek.

She giggles. They're both dressed like golfers, each wearing sunglasses. The school bus pulls up to their bumper. More cars file in behind us.

The twelve-gauge is loaded with five shells and already racked. I shift into park and take my foot off the brake. Al Green has a beautiful voice. The old couple is listening to a talk station.

I rest the muzzle on the edge of my driver's side window. The street light's green arrow has expired and traffic now crosses the intersection ahead of us. I lift the stock and aim the barrel at the woman's beehive hairdo. She turns and sees me, and her mouth becomes an O. I squeeze the trigger. Her whole head turns red. The gun kicks like karate. The old man is a howling baboon, cradling her body. I open the door and step out of the Beamer. I rack the gun and shoot him through the neck.

Horns blare.

Cars bang into each other, trying to speed away.

The school bus rumbles in reverse, smashing into the car behind it. I rack the gun and go for its door.

The lady bus driver reaches for the control lever to keep me out. The shotgun blasts apart the glass between us. I wedge open the door with the gun stock and force my way through. The screams of children chime through the cab. Some average-joe hero is rushing into the bus, but I toss him the driver's body like a boxing bag, and the man tumbles back outside. I peg the go-pedal and rip through the gears. The bus rams past the convertible and jumps the curb. We rumble over the median and roar down the road; it's the expressway or bust. Holy crap, I already hear sirens!

A school bus engine can pack upward of 300 horsepower, and can move a lot faster than you'd think if you don't give a damn about the cargo aboard.

"Mister, are you going to hurt us?" asks a pug-nosed little girl in the overhead mirror.

"Probably."

"Why'd you shoot Mrs. Hinklemeyer?" sniffles a gap-toothed chubby kid.

"I hated her name." I keep the gun right beside me, where they can see it.

"Why are you doin' this to us?"

"Because y'all are a bunch of nobodies," I tell him. "And so am I. But I've got a plan to change all that."

We hit the interstate. That's when I hear it—the sweet sound of beating mechanical wings. The thrum of helicopter blades is rising in the distance. The eye in the sky is on its way, 'cause baby I've hit the big time now.

"What kind of plan?" asks the tiny princess in the seat behind me.

I meet her puffy eyes in the mirror. "A plan to make us all famous. See, I've had a really bad day, but I plan to wrap it up on a high note. Today we all started out as nobodies, me and you both, darling. But by tomorrow, each and every one of you kids will be celebrated all over TV. Everybody'll know who you are. And everybody's going to know my name too."

I've got nothing against these kids, but I've got an omelet to make.

The other cars are falling away to give passage to the battalion of police cruisers and SUVs roaring up fast. I hear the chopper right above me, slicing the air to shingles, and there's a broadcast news van chasing up the rear.

I roll up on a tiny red SmartCar. A ridiculous thing. I make a hard right on top of it. Like a pinball paddle the bus sends it hurtling, and the cop cruisers scatter to avoid collision. I careen to an off-ramp, a swooping uphill climb to an overpass bridge. I'm stabbing the gas and grinding the gears to keep the clunky yellow box up to speed. The children are crying, but we're almost to the top.

Damn the brakes; we fly through the intersection. I decide there's no bridge in our future and steer for the peak. We're headed for the sweet spot between the overpass and the embankment.

The cops are trying to communicate through some sort of bullhorn. They're calling to me. They announce my name on the loudspeaker. Great balls of fire! They know my name! We leave the road, and the bus is one loud, long scream, as it launches into the air, casting a great black shadow over the cars passing on the lanes below.

Maybe I failed as a husband. Maybe I never became a big-shot in life. But I know at this one spectacular moment I've finally achieved something significant. Something a lot of people won't soon forget.

Like it or not, baby, I've become *somebody*.

The Red Card

Caroline found the greeting card in the kitchen after spending her first night in the apartment. She noticed it as she prepared her morning coffee. She could not imagine who might have left it, since few people knew her new address and she had invited no one to visit. The card, so deeply red it was almost maroon, stood on the white tiled kitchen island and partially open like a book on display.

Caroline poured a steaming cup of joe, added a dollop of milk (but never sugar), and leaned over the countertop on her elbows. She picked up the card and opened it to a stark white interior that stated in a black serif typeface:

`You will die in three days.`

A cough choked her and splashed the coffee, burning her wrist. Caroline set down the dripping mug and unrolled a paper towel.

Who the hell jokes like that? Nothing funny about a death threat.

After cleaning the spill, she stared at the card with contempt. It now lay flat and closed on the island and seemed to suck the light from the room. She compiled a mental police lineup, determined to match up motive with opportunity to leave the card. But nothing made sense. Newly single, she'd only arrived in town yesterday. Her ex-fiancé, Bob Neumeier, remained in Tuscaloosa with the Bitch Who Will Not Be Named. Besides, neither of those two were the vindictive type; after all, what's to be mad about? They now had each other.

Caroline's only local acquaintances were Mr. and Mrs. Walden. He was an older gentleman who hired Caroline to run his boutique so he could spend more time caring for his ailing wife. On her second job interview, Caroline had also met one of the sales associates, a college student named Jules, but she'd appeared only vaguely interested in the new store manager while acutely interested in her own cell phone.

Caroline knew none of these people with enough familiarity to elicit a threat or a bad practical joke.

She bit her lower lip. This card hadn't materialized out of the ether. No, an explanation definitely existed, of that she was certain. Unlike Bob and his religious fantasies, Caroline existed in the Real World of reason and logic. This meant someone had intruded into her dwelling on the very first night she called it home.

Could it be the landlord? A neighbor?

Suddenly, every closed door and blind corner in the apartment hid mysterious danger. Just out of sight lurked a knife-wielding killer … or a gun-carrying rapist…

Caroline reined in her imagination, but pulled a chef's knife from a kitchen drawer. With the blade held tightly in front of her, she crept down the hallway, peering cautiously into each room. In the bathroom, she pulled back the shower curtain with the knife-point aimed and ready. She detected no odd noises, nor saw anything out of place. She swept back down the hallway, clearing each room and checking every closet.

This intrusion simply would not stand, but for the moment, Caroline had no time to solve the riddle. Today was Wednesday and her first day to manage the store at Walden Fashions, so she'd have to take the questions and suspicions with her to work.

***

Mr. Walden, elderly and soft-spoken, left shortly after greeting Caroline with her own set of store keys. Throughout the shift, she kept a watchful eye on Jules. Business was slow, so the teenager spent much of her time giggling with friends over the phone, texting, and snapping selfies while she smiled or pouted. Jules' behavior struck Caroline as so shallow and banal that she decided the girl lacked the ingenuity or resourcefulness to pull off the card scheme.

A few ladies from town wandered through the shop, perusing the blouses and gowns. Caroline introduced herself, and took great effort to learn their names and faces, knowing that hospitality and personal charisma sold as much apparel as a trending style or a good sale.

A few men from neighboring shops stopped to say hello. A cute old man named Mr. Burnside introduced himself as owner of the town's only bookstore. A pimple-faced delivery driver brought Caroline a "welcome to town" pizza from the Slice of Heaven. Apparently the arrival of a new-hire in the shops of the Main Street Plaza amounted to a big event for the everyday workers.

Trapper Valley impressed her as a nice, quiet town, even quaint, but also a little commonplace and boring. The townsfolk greeted her with pleasant smiles and polite platitudes, and she graciously returned the gestures while eliminating each person from her list of possible suspects.

And this frustrating assessment made the mystery of the red card all the more vexing and pressing in her mind. Had she been targeted randomly?

Maybe it was a fluke. Maybe some wise-guy on the landlord's cleaning crew had left it on the island. Or maybe one of the movers she'd hired. And although she thought it highly unlikely that she'd missed seeing the card yesterday when moving into the apartment, she supposed it was technically possible, and settling on that idea calmed her nerves considerably more than dwelling on the prospect of a murderous intruder.

Caroline resolved to accept this idea—a prank from a worker—
and to put the matter out of her mind completely. Doing so would
make it much easier to sleep at night.

***

Caroline awoke to the rousing glow of morning sunshine
slicing through the blinds beside her bed. She sat up, yawned and
stretched, then slid into her slippers and headed to the kitchen for
a cup of coffee.

The sight of the card hit her like a slap. Standing upright and
halfway open, the same bottomless red like a vat of blood, it
occupied the very spot where she'd found it yesterday.

Last night she'd thrown the thing out. She'd dropped it into a
sack of trash, shoving it deep inside a pile of coffee grinds and
packing peanuts, then tightened the drawstring and hauled the
whole mess to the apartment complex's community dumpster at
the edge of the parking lot.

Still, there stood the card. Right on the island. Or, *a* card, she
reasoned. It could not be the *same* card. Either way meant the
intruder had returned.

The hairs on Caroline's neck prickled.

Again, she snatched the knife from the kitchen drawer. Its long,
sharp blade was meant for chopping vegetables, but she figured
it'd open a man's throat before he had a chance to put his hands on
her.

She grabbed the card, backed into a corner of the kitchen and
thumbed it open. In black serif typeface, it read:

`You will die in two days.`

Silently she listened to everything around her. The thrum of
the air conditioner. A car passing outside. The bark of a dog in the
distance. She heard no breathing but her own, no shuffling
movement or footsteps.

Her five senses said she was alone, but some other instinct
warned that she was not.

"Why are you doing this to me?" she demanded. "Who are you and what do you want?" The words were meant for anyone present, whoever they were.

But *was* anyone present? If nobody was here, then she was speaking to herself, and that was a crazy thing to do.

As she lay down the card, it stung the webbing of her thumb. She flipped up her palm to find the thin red line of a paper cut. She sucked out the blood.

Caroline stalked through the house in a huff, room by room, deciding to stab first and ask questions later. Anyone who'd pull this type of bullshit would get what they deserve.

But after an exhaustive search, the place appeared empty. Nobody home in the lonely apartment but Caroline. And it was time for Caroline to go to work.

***

A greater number of customers came into the boutique that morning. They browsed and touched the garments and peeked at price tags. Occasionally a lady would disappear into the fitting room or ask about extra sizes kept in the back stock room. Caroline quietly evaluated each person who crossed the threshold, searching for leering eyes or stolen glances, the slightest slip of disguise which might betray secret intent. After work, she continued her silent reconnaissance at the supermarket, the gas station, the drug store and the Frosty Parlor, where she stopped for frozen yogurt on the way home. Caroline, who considered herself a fairly shrewd judge of character, saw nothing in the face of anyone in Trapper Valley to suggest they might torment her with death threats.

Her tormentor had the upper hand. Someone was toying with her and seemingly had the ability to hide anywhere at any given time, inside the house or maybe just outside, and could spring a lethal attack at any moment. Sure, maybe the intruder was only getting their jollies from the sheer fear the warnings evoked, but without evidence to the contrary Caroline knew only a fool would fail to prepare for the worst.

After her last spoonful of raspberry yogurt, Caroline headed back toward the town square. She made two more stops.

At the Trapper Valley Police Station she filed a harassment report. A policeman told her they had very little to go on but claimed they took such threats seriously, and a cruiser would patrol past her house on special detail throughout the night. The officer's response sounded very detached and workmanlike to Caroline, but she wanted to get an official complaint on paper. That way, should she call the cops while screaming bloody murder in the night, maybe they would make her a top priority.

The second stop took her to a home electronics store, where she bought two wireless security cameras. The surveillance cameras would interface with software on her laptop for wireless remote recording. Caroline could even program an alarm to sound from her computer if the cameras captured motion during the night.

With their compact size and lightweight design, they could be mounted to virtually any smooth surface with peel-and-stick adhesive pads. Caroline stuck one on the kitchen wall and aimed it at the island. She stuck the other in the front foyer, aiming it at the front door into the apartment. The only other door led to a small balcony on the third floor of the building, which she dead-bolted.

Satisfied that the system was fully operational, she relaxed in her bed, pulled the sheet over her shoulders, and tried to get some sleep.

***

A red card awaited Caroline in the kitchen the next morning. The sight of it standing on the island sent an icy chill coursing through her body, riddling her skin with gooseflesh.

Yesterday, she'd wadded the card into a tiny ball and dumped it with the trash, which meant this card was new and that the intruder had returned.

Yet, she'd heard no alarm from the security system. She could even see the interior chain undisturbed on the front door.

With trembling fingers, she reached for the card and opened to its bright interior.

`You will die tomorrow.`

A scream rose in Caroline's throat, a scream that germinated from a deeply seeded fear but then grew and spread like a sprawling vine which finally burst from her mouth in a raging fury. Someone, whoever it was, had gone too far. No more Ms. Nice Girl.

She snatched the chef's knife and loped from room to room ready to slash and stab. The balcony door remained locked. The apartment showed no signs of entry, and she found nobody on the premises, just like she'd grimly expected.

Caroline stormed into her bedroom, plopped onto the mattress and unfolded the laptop to the security app. As she reviewed the night's video feed, she caught sight of the red card on the kitchen island. The time on the video read 2:35 am.

She jogged the video backward. At 1:55 the island was bare, showing no card. She nudged the digital ticker at the bottom of the video box, and the picture jumped ahead. At 2:20, she saw the card. At 2:15, she saw nothing.

Incrementally, Caroline moved the video back and forth until she pinpointed 2:17:34, where the frame depicted no card on the island. In the next frame, an odd disruption obscured the picture, a split-second break in the video in which fuzzy digital waves flashed across the screen, then vanished to reveal the red card standing there like a knife wound against the white porcelain. Between 2:17:34 and 2:17:36 the card had appeared from thin air at the very same instant the video camera malfunctioned, and Caroline's unquestioning certainty that there's *no freaking way* that could actually happen renewed her with fresh hot fury. This meant that not only did someone keep intruding in an attempt to scare her, but now they'd escalated their harassment to a whole new level. Someone had tinkered with the camera.

Maybe... she thought. *Maybe someone is trying to get me to crack up. Maybe someone is trying to get me to believe the unbelievable. Because believing in things that don't exist is what crazy people do. And crazy people are much easier to dismiss, to marginalize, than a strong woman with a sound mind.*

Caroline had Lorraine's phone number written on a pad of paper in her purse. It had showed up on Bill's mobile months ago, and she'd grown suspicious. She didn't know why she'd kept track of it after the breakup, but now was glad that she had. She dialed it.

"Lorraine," Caroline said to the voice who picked up on the other end.

"This is she," the lady said. "Who is this?"

"I think you know who this is."

"Mmmm, no. I don't think so. How can I help..."

The way she trailed off told Caroline that Lorraine realized who was calling. "That's right," she said. "It's Caroline Renner. And I'd like to know just what the hell you and Bob are trying to pull."

Bob Neumeier was hopelessly square and typically compassionate, so Caroline found it difficult to believe he would initiate this type of harassment—which meant Lorraine had concocted the whole scheme.

"Caroline? I'm sorry, Caroline, but I don't know what you're talking about."

"*I don't know what you're talking about...*" Caroline mocked in a squeaky, childish voice and hated her own immaturity, even as the words left her mouth. Still, she plowed ahead. "Believe me, that's exactly what I expected you to say. Because you want to plant doubt in my mind. That's the whole point, right? You want to get inside my head. But I've got news, Lorraine. It's not going to work."

"Look. I don't know what you're going on about. Bob told me you had issues, but whatever you're talking about, you can bet it doesn't involve me in any way. And I do not appreciate being spoken to in this manner."

"You're going to break into my apartment and then—"

"Break into your apartment! What on earth are you talking about?" Lorraine said. "Look, if you have some sort of problem, then you really need to call Bob."

"I'm calling *you!* You're the bitch who wrecked my engagement! You got into his head and now you're trying to get into mine!"

"This is ridiculous. It was never going to work between you two. You're both too different. If you're going to start a family together, you have to share a foundation of belief. And you two didn't. He told you that. You knew what Bob valued in life and you didn't share it."

"Oh sure, your myths and fairytales. That's a fine foundation for raising a family."

"Call it whatever you want, Caroline. We call it *faith*. And yes, a shared belief structure is fundamental to a successful marriage. To raise children in a properly functional home."

"Believing in lies won't help anybody," Caroline said, confirming her suspicion. "That's what's going on, isn't it? This is some sad attempt to make me believe in bullshit, just like you two do."

"We're not attempting to do anything to you."

"Well, it won't work. I only believe what I can see. That's why you don't want me to see who's leaving the cards, isn't it? You want to make me to think that *nobody* is leaving the cards. That they just *magically* appear. You want me to believe in impossible things."

"Caroline, I don't know what you're talking about."

"You want me to believe in impossible things so you can say I'm *crazy*. Because nobody gives a damn about crazy people. They get ostracized so they don't matter anymore. And if I don't matter, then it makes it easier for you to live with yourself after what you did to me!"

"I'm hanging up the phone now."

"I know it's you, you *bitch!* I may not have seen you do it, but there's only two names on my list of suspects, and it's yours and Bob's!"

"Whatever. You need to get some help. Goodbye, Caroline."

With a click the line went dead.

Caroline tasted blood and realized with a stinging sensation she'd gnawed her fingernail to the quick while leaning against the wall with the dead phone pinched against her ear. She was unsure exactly how long she'd been standing there thinking of red cards, thinking of Bob and Lorraine, and of strange phenomena that always had logical explanations, yet teased and antagonized her by evading her grasp.

She wrapped a Band-Aid around her index finger, got ready for work and drove to Walden Fashions while her head spun and simmered with hate.

The morning passed with a gray dullness. A drizzling rain kept most customers away, and Jules tended to the few who showed up. Caroline felt this was best since she was so distracted by her righteous anger and a weird sense of dread. She reasoned the whole ordeal had to come to a head soon because, according to the card, either she would die tomorrow—*come and try it, bitch!*—or she would not. And by not dying, she'd have proven the whole thing to be the scam she knew it to be. The jig would be up, and this whole ugly chapter of her life a fading memory.

The only loose end seemed to be the unknown level of dedication that Lorraine or Bob (or whoever) had to their little campaign of terror. What if they were fully committed to the idea? What if it wasn't Bob or Lorraine, but someone else, and they actually intended to murder her?

The unanswered questions rattled around her mind all day like pebbles in a paint can, and clear thoughts were scarce.

Caroline took a late lunch break. She walked down the plaza to Triple-A Guns and Pawn. She picked out a snub-nose .38 revolver, passed a background check, and returned to her apartment that evening as an armed woman.

***

Before loading the bullets, Caroline spent a while getting to know the gun, aiming at herself in the mirror. She would cock the hammer, align the sight with the muzzle reflecting back at her, and steadily squeeze the trigger until she heard the metallic click. She was no pro, but this was not her first time around a firearm. Bob owned a nine-millimeter, and they'd taken a few hikes into the woods where they shot at paper targets. More than just comfortable, Caroline was confident with the weapon.

As midnight drew near, she phoned her parents and had a warm chat with both, wishing them the best and professing her love, never hinting that something might trouble her. She hung up with a tear in her eye.

She then speculated when a confrontation might go down. The strike of twelve would push tonight into tomorrow, and any time in the following twenty-four hours would be ripe for attack if some low-life were to make good on the threat. She had twenty-four hours to stay alive, to get to the other side of this big black hole which had opened in her life. To prove it all a hoax, or to defend herself from a killer.

It would be a long night, if she were lucky.

Tempted by a glass of wine, she instead poured ice water and settled into the sofa with a blanket for an *Andy Griffith Show* rerun—something cheerful to keep her mind occupied. The pistol never left her lap. The security cameras were active, the doors were secure, and she'd rigged both with a long strip of round metal bells she'd retrieved from a box of Christmas decorations. Anyone opened them and she'd hear the chimes, aim the gun and then it's, *"Night-night Mr. Hallmark, now your family can expect some cards of their own—condolence cards."*

But when 11:59 rolled into 12:00am with the eerie chime of a wall clock, the night assumed an air of creeping hostility despite Caroline's best efforts to remain skeptical. Every light in the apartment shined from white bulbs, but even the antics of Goober and Barney Fife couldn't brighten the black shadows which loomed outside and hid things that did not want to be seen.

Someone on TV was selling a miracle-working electric grill on a looping commercial as 1:44 stretched into 2:30. Caroline's every nerve hummed, and she made periodic patrols throughout the apartment, the gun hot in her sweating palm.

Sleep was out of the question.

At 6:30, she decided her aspiring murderer must not be a morning person, so she went to the kitchen for coffee and eggs.

The sight of a new card sent a spear of ice through her mind, past her heart and into her bladder, and she had a sudden urge to pee. The thing seared her eyes like a burning ember, mocking her, ridiculing her sense of reason. She grinded her teeth and charged throughout the house, waving the gun and cursing, in demand of blood and death. Beyond the intrusion, beyond the threats, it was the insult to her intelligence that Caroline ultimately refused to abide. She refused to believe the impossible was really possible, and this attempt to drive her crazy would never work because Caroline had made a decision. She planned to end the harassment by killing whatever dirtbag had engineered this hellish scheme, no matter what reasons they might claim to have. This decision was not negotiable. They'd gone too far this time, and at first sight she was going to blow out their brains—before they succeeded in pushing her beyond the brink of sanity.

Case closed.

If she caught them inside her house—even if unarmed and they somehow proved they never meant actual harm—Caroline resolved to still shoot them and plead self-defense.

She tipped the card open with the barrel of her gun. It read:

```
Just a few hours left.
```

Caroline heard laughter. High and hysterical guffaws shouted with brainless abandon. After a moment she realized it was her own voice, and shut up.

Again, she found the security video useless.

She phoned the police and told her story. They sent over a young, handsome officer with broad shoulders, who nodded sympathetically and said he understood. With Caroline's blessing, he searched the premises as she'd done a million times, and he proved equally unsuccessful at finding a clue. He vowed to conduct regular patrols past the property throughout the day, and then he left.

Only fifteen hours to go, Caroline assured herself as she passed from the hallway into the kitchen on patrol of her own.

There, on the island, stood a new red card.

She nearly leapt to the ceiling at the shrill ring of her mobile. Stunned, she stood gawking at the card as the phone buzzed in her pocket. Finally, she answered.

"Caroline," spoke a familiar voice.

"Bob," she said from somewhere far away.

"Caroline, Lorraine called me. What the heck is going on?" The anger in his voice snatched her back to earth.

"Nice timing, Bob. Is that what you planned? Are you monitoring me to know when I find the cards?"

"I don't know what you're—"

"I'm not an idiot, Bob, and I'm not insane. And you're not going to convince me otherwise."

"Nobody's trying to convince you of anything. Frankly, I'm worried. You sound as disturbed as Lorraine described."

"*Ha!*" She belted out the laugh like it should be coupled with a judo chop. "That's a riot. So you're Mr. Altruistic all of sudden? I don't buy it. I think you're trying to convince me to believe in things that don't exist. To believe in impossible things, like you do. But I'm not falling for it. Because I only believe what I see to be a fact."

"I'm sorry about what happened between us. But if you're going to be hostile, then it's best you just leave us alone. Don't call Lorraine."

"Seeing is believing, Bob."

"You need to see a psychiatrist."

"Seeing is believing. And if I see you in my apartment, I'm going to kill you."

"Is that a threat?"

"No, Bob," said Caroline. "That's a promise."

The line went dead.

She opened the card, which read:

`You die at noon.`

Caroline dropped it, and the paper floated to the floor like a dying cardinal.

Seeing is believing.

Frantically, Caroline ripped the drawers from the kitchen island. Silverware clanged to the porcelain floor. She threw open the cabinet doors and searched through the pots and pans and Tupperware. She had investigated the kitchen many times, but felt compelled to do it again, to scour the place exhaustively to find some sort of surveillance device. Or any hidden apparatus that would explain the placement of the cards. She must have missed something. There must be an explanation, because absolutely nothing else made sense. So, Caroline rummaged through everything stored anywhere in the kitchen—the pantry, the dishwasher, the refrigerator and freezer—and hurled it all onto the floor. Finding nothing, she tore apart the rest of the apartment as well, room by room and closet by closet. She unscrewed air vent registers and tried to remove the bathroom mirror but the damn thing was glued in place. She glared at her reflection with boiling contempt and wondered what lay on the other side, possibly obscured by special one-way glass.

By the time 11:45 rolled around, exhaustion had taken its toll. Caroline's home turned against her. Each door squeaked out a laugh at her when she opened it. The low roar of the water heater was a crowd of hushed voices murmuring behind her back. The cabinet hinges grimaced at her with screws for eyes and interlocking knuckles for clenched teeth. Even the electrical receptacles all had two noseless faces that moaned a mournful song about people who had lost their minds.

Caroline poured a fresh cup of joe. She added a dollop of cream (but never sugar) and took comfort in the warmth as the coffee ran down her throat. She turned to find a new card on the island.

With calm resignation, she picked it up and opened it.

`Ten minutes to go.`

A smile stretched across Caroline's face, but she didn't know why. She then found herself carefully stepping over the clutter in the kitchen and walking down the hallway. She stepped into the bathroom and looked in the mirror at her wild-eyed face and its hysterical grin. She lifted the coffee mug, gave a fierce shriek and launched it into the glass. With calamitous racket, shards of mirror rained down onto the sink and vanity. Much of the mirror remained stuck to the drywall, and Caroline used her nails to pry off the fragments to see behind them. The jagged edges sliced her fingertips, which left red smears on the wall.

She found nothing hidden beyond the mirror.

Stumbling back into the kitchen, she found yet another new card resting on the island.

With trembling fingers she opened to the white inside. It carried the shortest message yet.

`Five minutes, Caroline.`

The room listed with a dreamlike quality, the walls bending outward as though seen through a fish-eye lens. She so badly needed sleep, or just a moment to rest and clear her swimming head, but she had such a little way to go.

Caroline rubbed her eyes and steadied herself. She realized this new card had been the first to be personalized. Appropriate, she thought, since they'd gotten to know each other so well—these cards and her.

Time to take care of business. She lifted the .38 from the island and cocked the hammer. With her eyes crawling over every inch of the apartment, Caroline made her way into the living room. The windowless corner with the TV would provide cover from behind so she could keep all other points of entry—and avenues of attack—in clear view. She backed against it with the pistol raised.

The place was quiet. Only the whir of the air conditioner stirred the calm. And then the hum of an automobile passing outside.

Something on the entertainment center caught her view. A red card stood next to the television, where she could swear it had not existed only seconds ago.

With the pistol still raised Caroline grabbed the card and opened it. Two words:

`One minute.`

A chirp of laughter escaped her. A strange thrill coursed through Caroline, and her heartbeat shifted into a higher gear. She supposed that under the right circumstances adrenaline could get a person high, and she was now flying. In less than sixty seconds, it would all be over. Either nothing would happen, the threat would be proven a hoax, and she could stop dreading her murder. Or, someone would show up, maybe Bob or Lorraine—hopefully both—and Caroline would fill them with hot lead. And she looked forward to the joy of the justified kill.

The seconds stretched and lingered, but finally the clock on the wall gave its eerie chime and bonged out twelve deep tones to indicate noon had arrived.

Time for the axe to fall.

But Bob and Lorraine did not storm through the doors. A SWAT team of secret stalkers didn't crash through the windows and cut her to ribbons. Nothing happened. Another minute passed.

Caroline saw nothing out of the ordinary. She saw no threat whatsoever.

A chuckle rose from deep in her belly. "I beat you," she said softly, "I beat you bastards." Her voice gained strength. "*I* win! Not you!"

No reply came from anywhere.

"I *knew* this was a lie!" Caroline shouted to the empty apartment and the world around her. "I'm still standing! Past the deadline! And I don't see my 'killer' anywhere. I'm still alive and I don't see a damn thing that's going to change that! I don't see a thing, and seeing is believing!" She set the pistol down and lifted the red card above her head. "*Seeing is believing!*"

Caroline pinched the card between her fingertips, belted out a primal scream and ripped it in half.

Her stomach cramped fiercely. Tight abdominal pressure bloated within and pierced her gut. The room spun around, yet Caroline's feet remained fixed. The muscles of her back stretched and frayed, then tendons snapped from bones with popping noises. The crunch of twisting spine rumbled through her back as she floated downward, the walls swirling and sideways. The tile floor came up fast.

Caroline's nose exploded with blood and agony on impact.

From the cold porcelain floor, she forced her eyes open and stared in awe at her blue-jeaned legs, which stood above her, still attached to her pelvis, although no body remained above the waistline. The legs listed toward her, pulled by the entrails that stretched up from her torso in a thick, dripping bundle. Her bottom half tilted and fell to the floor, spilling a stew of offal into the pond of warm blood which spread beneath Caroline and leached into her hair and T-shirt. She gasped from deep in her throat but drew no air into her lungs.

With her vision flashing in and out, brightly then darkly like a shorting circuit, Caroline tried desperately to take in her surroundings. She was alone, but torn to pieces. Nothing in sight could explain the savagery, and the absurdity of what had happened gripped Caroline's mind and sunk its fangs deep inside, rending apart everything she conceived as possible.

As the hard angles of the room softened and warped around her, and every straight line bent and wavered, Caroline's head rolled to the side and she spotted a new red card. It stood on the floor not two feet away, partly open like a book on display, blending almost perfectly with the crimson pooling around it.

She summoned the last vestiges of dying strength and inched her hand toward it, dragging her elbow behind crawling fingers. At last she reached the thing, pinched it between her fingertips and opened it.

In a black serif typeface the card asked a simple question:
See?

The Neighbor at the Curb

Lois Bishop paced her living room, cooing into Polly's ear. Polly was teething, and her constant crying had gone on for days. As a working mother, Lois hated the idea of dropping off her ailing daughter at daycare each morning, but the incessant whining was proving to be just as much a burden as the guilt.

"Come on, Maya, we're late!" she called down the hallway to her older daughter. At five years old, Maya now insisted on brushing her own teeth, which Lois encouraged, but it always seemed to take a half-hour to do it.

The baby whimpered, and Lois hugged her tightly. If only she could take away Polly's aches and pains. The Orajel she'd been applying might as well have been tap water for all the good it was doing.

Somewhere up the road Lois heard the mechanical roar of a garbage truck. On Tuesdays, her husband John often forgot to take the trash bin to the curb before going to work, which would leave her one more responsibility to add to the stack. She carried Polly to the second-level window overlooking the street and twisted the rod that opened the blinds. The can stood at the curb. Good job, John.

A neighborhood cat passed the waste bin, gave it a sniff, and continued its way down the street. Mr. Burnside, the next-door neighbor, drove past in his station wagon as he headed to work at the book store.

Hal Clement from across the street had also pulled a bin to the edge of his driveway. The lid hung open and it looked half full. Hal now carried another load across the lawn to the can. He lifted the bundle before him with both hands, and it squirmed. With little arms and a swiveling head, the flailing child in Hal's arms wiggled and kicked as he neared the waste bin. He hoisted the child high, then crammed it into the trash.

Lois lost her breath. *My God! Little April!*

The tot struggled in the bin, but her father stuffed her back down and slammed the lid, sealing her in darkness.

Lois' muscles went rigid, but her mind swooped down a tunnel of confusion and disbelief. Had Hal lost his mind? He and John were fishing buddies. Their families barbecued together.

His face red with fury, Hal clenched the lid closed on the bin as he looked left and right, presumably for witnesses. He wore a gray jogging suit, and his beefy shoulders heaved with agitated breathing.

Lois knew his wife Sandra would be flipping out. So where the hell was Sandra?

"Mom, I'm done! I used the SpongeBob toothpaste!"

Lois heard Maya's words, but the meaning didn't sink in and only settled somewhere on the surface where the morning still made sense. She closed the blinds for fear Hal might look up and see her. Then she slightly reopened them to confirm what she'd seen. Her burly neighbor, still hovering over the bin, spat onto the ground and muttered something to himself. Then he turned and stalked back to his house. The front door slammed behind him.

Lois fixed on the Clements' waste bin. The container shook. The lid lifted slightly, only to fall back down. A sickly sensation festered in her stomach, like she'd eaten spoiled meat.

"Time to go to school?" Maya appeared in the doorway wearing blue jeans and a red t-shirt adorned with a Wonder Woman emblem.

"No," Lois said, her brain racing. "Not now. Maya, I need you to do me a favor. I need to you to watch Polly for a minute. Can you do that for just a minute? I have to go across the street."

"Awww," Maya pleaded. "Where are you going? I want to go."

"No, I need you to watch your sister like a big girl." Lois stepped to the couch and set blonde-haired Polly between two pillows. As soon as she released her, Polly erupted into another crying fit. "I'll be right back."

Lois stepped onto her front porch and tingled with surreal paranoia. This bright spring day, pleasantly mild with a slight breeze and scented with blooming wildflowers, hid some unseen malevolence which clashed with her routine world of workday tedium. Seeing what she'd seen had tilted the earth's axis. This was normally a quiet neighborhood, and the Clements had always been reasonable people. Now nothing was normal, and the act of crossing the street to rescue little April made her feel oddly like an intruder.

Her heels clicked across the asphalt. She had to make this fast. The Clement house had its curtains drawn. If Hal was watching, she couldn't see him. Muffled sobs met her ears as she drew close to the bin.

She lifted the lid. The big plastic cap flipped back on its hinges. The baby girl looked up at Lois, her face flushed from bawling. Coffee grounds and dryer lint clung to her cheeks and arms. The crying soared. Lois lifted April out by the shoulders and pulled her close.

What she saw further down in the bin struck her like a thunderbolt: A face looked up from the garbage and winked. At least, part of a face.

The earth spun. Lois staggered backward. She braced herself on the garbage bin, then released it again in revulsion.

Get back home!

She set sights on her front porch, regained footing, and marched homeward with the baby.

Oh, Sandra…

The face hadn't been winking. Half buried in the trash, Sandra had been missing an eye. One of her eyes had stared out at nothing, but the other socket was empty—only a ragged red hole, like someone had scooped out a peach pit.

Keep it together, Lois.

The short trek across the street dragged on her like she trudged through a marsh. That ghastly image kept plaguing her mind. Sandra's tongue, torn and distended, had lolled from her mouth as though wrenched out with pliers.

Don't think about it.

Was only Sandra's head in the waste bin, or had Hal stuffed her whole body down into the garbage? Lois hadn't looked long enough to see, yet she'd seen far too much.

She grabbed the front door handle, threw it open and stumbled inside her house. Kissing April on the forehead, she turned around in the foyer as Hal stepped from his house onto his front stoop. He stood stone-faced, arms straight at his sides, and locked eyes with Lois from across the street. She slammed the door.

Lois twisted the lock. Throwing the deadbolt, she dashed to the other doors of the lower level to lock them too. April's shrill crying kept ringing in her ear throughout it all. Polly's screaming echoed it from upstairs.

"Mommy," Maya called from the top of the staircase. "Polly won't stop throwing a fit!"

"Be there in a minute, honey!" Lois rushed through the kitchen but did not see her cell phone. No sign of it in the bathroom, either. She trampled up the stairs.

"Maya, have you seen my phone?"

On the couch, Maya pranced a toy horse before her bawling sister in a futile attempt to entertain. She looked at her mother. "Is that April?"

With both babies crying together, the noise doubled.

"Yes," Lois said, trying to maintain a calm demeanor and not alarm the children. "Have you seen my phone?"

"I was playing a game on it."

"Well, go get it! Fast! I need it! *Chop-chop!*"

Maya hopped up and scurried out of the room.

A heavy thud boomed from the lower floor. Lois's heart sank. Then another impact thundered from below, and she knew with a grim certainty that Hal Clement was trying to force his way through her front door.

"Maya, hurry!"

"I'm looking for it!'

Lois squatted down, scooped up Polly with her free hand, and strained to straighten back up with the double load. She carried the girls over to the top of the stairs, within view of the front door. The sidelite to the left of the entry darkened as a shadow passed it. With another pounding, the door buckled, but still held.

"The phone, Maya!"

"I found it!"

"Dial 9-1-1!"

"Okay!"

Focus, Lois. Think. If he breaks through that door, he's heading straight up the stairs, and you've got to have a plan to keep the kids safe.

"Are you dialing? Is it ringing?" she called over her shoulder.

"I'm dialing!" Maya shouted. Lois had taught her about the emergency number.

From somewhere outside came a different bang—the closing of a car door, and then a man's voice. Lois sidestepped down the hall and back to the living-room window. A car idled on the street in front of the house. A thin man in a long-sleeved buttoned shirt came around the side of the vehicle while shielding his eyes from the sun with his hand. He appeared to be addressing Hal on Lois' front lawn. She could not discern the exchange but thought she made out the words *"some kind of problem."*

The man then dropped his hand and switched his stance. She recognized Mr. Farmer, the appliance repairman from a block away. He turned around and dashed back toward his vehicle. He nearly slipped on the asphalt but caught himself on the trunk of his car. He pulled himself up and scrambled for the driver's door. But a rolling gray boulder in the form of Hal Clement barreled into him and crushed Mr. Farmer against the side mirror.

"My god!" Lois cried, and Maya said something in response which got lost in the storm between Lois' ears.

Mr. Farmer tried to punch and struggle, but Hal outweighed him by at least sixty pounds. He bashed the skinny neighbor against the door of the old Camry with his thick forearm. Then he clutched Mr. Farmer by the chin and scalp and rammed his face into the window. Hal hauled him back and smashed the man's face again, and this time pieces of glass burst out like glitter.

Lois clenched her fists so tightly her palms stung. The screaming of the children shook her to the core, like air-raid sirens. Maya joined her at the window.

Mr. Farmer swayed limply on his feet. Hal slammed his head onto the car's roof before releasing him. The beaten man slid to the ground on the far side of the Camry. Hal opened the car door, kicked something on the ground, then slammed the door against it. An obstacle between the door and the car frame—Mr. Farmer— prevented him from closing it all the way. Hal pulled back the door then slammed it, pulled it back again then slammed it.

"Why is Mr. Clement hurting that man, Mommy?"

Lois heard the pain in her voice. "Don't look, honey."

Maya stopped watching and buried her face in her mother's blouse.

"The police…" *Keep your head together, Lois.* "Maya, did you call 9-1-1?"

Her daughter mumbled through tears and fabric, "I tried but it wouldn't work."

A quick glance out the window showed Hal stalking across the street to his house and opening the door.

Lois stepped away from her. "Maya. Where is the phone?"

Maya walked to the recliner and lifted it from the armrest. "I kept pressing the numbers."

Lois knelt down and put the babies on the carpeted floor in the corner of the room. She took the phone and read the glowing characters *9-1-1-X*. The mobile required a four-digit security code to access its calling feature, and Maya hadn't entered it. Her attempts to call hadn't worked. Lois tapped the code onto the screen and dialed the emergency number.

The connection came quickly. "Nine-one-one. What's your emergency?"

"Murder! My god, there's been a murder—no, *two* murders!"

"I understand," assured a steady female voice. "Okay, remain calm. Where are you?"

A small Kia hatchback pulled up behind Mr. Farmer's Camry.

"I'm at 1630 Pinewood Lane in Trapper Valley."

The operator repeated the address back to her and asked, "What is your name?"

"This is Lois Bishop. I'm here with my two daughters. And I've got another little girl who lives across the street. I had to go get her from the trash because her father—" Lois stopped to catch her breath. She sniffed back mucus, unsure how long she'd been sobbing.

The driver of the Kia, a plump woman with her hair pulled back, stepped out of the vehicle and stood behind its door. She stared at the spot where Mr. Farmer had fallen.

"The father, Hal Clement, who lives across the street, killed his wife Sandra and tried to kill their baby. He also killed another neighbor right in front of us." She choked back a hiccupping sob.

Across the street, the door to the Clement house flew open. Lois froze.

Hal emerged from the dark entry bearing an axe.

"Don't hang up," the operator said. "Help is on the way."

"Oh my god. Oh my god, *Oh my god!*"

Raising the axe over his shoulder, Hal charged the woman driver. She hopped back into the car and had it shifted into reverse before her door was closed. Slicing through the air, the axe-blade missed completely as the car shot backwards. The tires chirped at the street corner. Momentum slung the Kia's door shut. The hatchback cut a sharp left, bucked forward and zoomed away.

Hal huffed and seethed, then turned his gaze to Lois' house. He stomped across the lawn while gripping the long wooden handle. As he neared the porch, she lost sight of him.

The instructions from the emergency operator were lost to a mental white noise while Lois envisioned her forthcoming death. Hal would soon splinter the wooden door, lunge up the staircase, corner her family and hack everyone to pieces. She had only a matter of minutes to stop it from happening.

"...whatever it takes to protect yourself and the children." Those were the final words Lois heard before dropping the phone to the floor.

"Maya, we're all going to your room." Lois scooped up the infants, whose strident fits had been momentarily replaced by mutual fascination as they pawed each others' faces.

Maya's bedroom shared a bathroom with Polly's. Beneath that bathroom window, and a little to the right, was a last resort for escape—a metal awning over a side door that would break their fall to the ground.

A loud cracking noise gripped Lois from downstairs.

"Bedroom! Now!" They jogged down the hall. Inside the room, she ordered Maya to lock the door. Lois nestled the two babies into the tub of the adjoining bathroom. She surrounded them with towels as makeshift blankets.

THWACK! Another blow sounded from the front door below.

Lois dashed over to the bedroom door and double-checked that Maya had locked it. The hollow-core slab wouldn't stop a man with an axe, but maybe it would slow him down. She scoured the room for a makeshift weapon but saw nothing practical.

THWACK! Her heart skipped a beat.

Maya wailed, "Is Mr. Clement coming to get us?!"

"Everything will be fine!" Lois marveled at the insanity of her own words.

She jerked open drawers and flung open a closet, rifling through Maya's clothes and toys. *What do you expect to find in a five-year-old's room? A loaded gun?*

THWACK-BOOM! The noise downstairs was followed by a metallic squeak and a hollow echo. Hal had broken through the front door.

"Maya, get in the bathroom!"

In a panic, Lois grabbed a wire coat hanger and dashed inside with the children. It occurred to her as she slammed the bathroom door, locked it, and pressed her back against it, that she must have gotten the coat-hanger notion from an old movie. Jamie Lee Curtis had used one to stab a killer in the eye when she'd been cornered in a closet. But that was a movie.

... And I'm no scream queen. And the killer in the movie hadn't been swinging an axe.

She dropped the hanger.

As it landed, the bathroom floor vibrated beneath her from heavy footfalls on the staircase. Lois flipped both latches on the window locks and snapped open the lower sash. She pushed away the screen and peered outside. A warm morning breeze rushed into the room. The top of the garage-door awning was only about five feet down. With a little sideways swing on the descent, Maya could make the drop safely then catch the babies as Lois tossed them out the window.

"Maya, I'm going to lower you down. I need you to hop onto that little roof outside, then hop down to the grass."

"Why, Mommy? Why is Mr. Clement chasing us?"

"He's very sick, Maya. Come to the window, I'll lift you up."

"I can't, Mommy, I'm scared!"

"Yes you can. And you *will*."

Both babies had rediscovered their capacity to shriek, and the hard tile walls amplified their piercing squeals.

Lois turned over a wastebasket to give Maya a foothold through the window.

"But *Mommmm*. I'm too scared! I don't want to—"

Lois grabbed Maya's face and squeezed. Her daughter's cheeks pinched together, and her deep brown eyes retreated with a terror Lois had never seen. She'd never seen it because she'd never laid a hand on Maya in anger, and now her daughter cowered in fear of her mother for the very first time. This recognition burned inside Lois like lye on a corpse. At that moment Maya feared *her*. Maybe feared her more than she feared the heights outside the window. Maybe even more than she feared the madman who'd just smacked an axe into her bedroom door.

Yet, although it tortured Lois to do it, she had to use that fear as a tool. She had to use it to get Maya outside, to save these children.

"The man outside is trying to hurt all of us. He's trying to *kill* your mother. You will do exactly as I say, and you will *not* talk back! Do you understand me?" She maintained a laser focus on Maya's pupils as she spoke those words, hoping to connect with her daughter on a deeper plane, some spiritual level Maya might reflect upon one day should Lois not make it out alive.

"I must be cruel only to be kind..." The old Shakespeare line rang from the memory of Lois' high school English class.

Maya nodded in slow motion, her lip quivering.

The blade of the axe crashed through the door of the bathroom. Lois watched the black metal wedge retreat to the other side of the gashed wood, and knew another blow was right behind it. She turned back to Maya who was now halfway out the window, inspired by the axe.

Lois clutched beneath her daughter's thin arms and leaned forward. Maya's legs kicked the siding as she slid outward and dangled from her grip.

CRACK! The bathroom shook as wood splinters littered the sink to her left.

"Here we go!" Lois swung Maya to the left then shifted momentum to the right, and released her. Maya's thigh hit the awning, and she tried to grip the edges but slid off the incline. She thumped to the ground on her side and cried out.

Lois spun to see a huge trench had been cut through the door. Hal Clement's hand groped inside for the doorknob. Lois grabbed the porcelain lid of the toilet tank. She ripped it loose and swung it in an overhead arc. The white slab slammed his fingers against the brass knob and broke into pieces. Hal reeled backward and bellowed from the other room.

"You're not getting these babies!" she roared through the door.

Polly's cheek against Lois' own felt so warm and soft as she gathered her youngest from the tub. At the window, she kissed her forehead and wished a quick prayer that she'd soon feel that warmth again.

"You ready, honey? I've got to drop her to you," she called to Maya, who dusted herself off.

"What if I drop her?"

"You won't. Now, here she comes." As Polly wiggled, Lois held her out the window in midair. Maya waited below with an expression of zero confidence.

Lois let go. Maya's arms closed around Polly. They both fell back onto the grass.

Thank you, God.

The wicker laundry hamper against the wall teemed with clothing, heavy from the packed fabric. Lois dragged it across the floor and pushed it over to help block the door.

Hal's face appeared through the gaping hole, dripping sweat and warped with rage. He brandished his weapon with two fists— a white-knuckle grip with his right hand, but two fingers on his left one bent outward at odd angles. Too bad Hal was right-handed. With a step backward, he lifted the axe high and mighty.

Lois shot over to April and gathered her up.

The black blade plunged through the door, breaking away a huge section of the plywood veneer and distorting the frame. The upper quarter collapsed inward, and Hal had easy access to the knob. He unlocked it and began slamming his knee against the lower portion of the ravaged door to scoot the hamper out of the way.

At the window, Lois held April outside, her forearms burning from the weight as she floated the child aloft while Maya readied for the catch. Lois released her. Maya grabbed April and tumbled to the ground.

With sirens blaring, two police cruisers zoomed down Pinewood Lane toward the house.

Lois returned to Hal as he extricated himself from the ruined wood slab to climb over the hamper. She dove at him and raked her nails across his face, cutting deep red lines. He jerked away then exploded back at her like TNT. The axe flew through the air one-handed.

Lois' forearm appeared before her as sheer thoughtless instinct, guarding her face and chest. That steel wedge snapped through it with ease. Something broke. Blood hit the wall. Forced backward, she stumbled against the counter but did not fall.

Lois lifted her left hand but saw only a pink stump. From the cleft flesh, two jagged white sticks protruded, one an inch longer than the other. She instantly became light as a feather, the floor like a cloud.

Hal snarled like an animal and stomped onto the hamper, the wicker crunching and popping as it caved beneath him.

The kids need you, Lois! The kids...

She steeled herself, reared back her mangled forearm and speared it forth. The sharp point of her broken radius skewered Hal right in the eye. It sank in deep.

That's for Sandra!

Hal screamed and clutched his bleeding face with his good hand. With the other arm flailing, his big frame fell back against the doorjamb, and then he shrank out of the room with a whimper.

A searing pain flashed through Lois. Not limited to the limb, the pulsing anguish coursed up her arm and overtook her in a wave. Her knees folded, and she struggled to remain afoot as a bout of nausea stirred inside her. She squinted hard and choked it back.

Her eyelids opened to a bathrobe hanging from a coat hook on the wall.

Grab it. Snatch the belt off it.

Lois did these things, which her mind commanded from some remote place within her.

Don't panic. Wrap the cloth around your arm to close off the artery. Just like you learned back in Girl Scouts. Bite one end with your teeth and tie a granny knot. Pull it tight.

The harried voices of the police blended with the crying of her children somewhere outside.

She applied the strip, and with a jerk of her jaws drew it taut. The steady flow of blood slowed to a trickle. She needed a stick—something stiff and oblong—to tighten the tourniquet and act as a valve handle. A blue toothbrush hung from a porcelain holder mortared to the wall. She grabbed it as Hal burst back through the door with his one working eye. Over the hamper he came, baring his teeth with axe in hand.

Lois slid the toothbrush upward from the holder. The tip of the handle remained enclosed in the hard porcelain. With a sharp twist of the wrist she snapped off the blunt end and made a plastic shiv.

Hal raised the axe and opened his mouth wide, like he meant to eat her as he chopped. But Lois ducked down and slipped beneath his arm. The axe-blade hacked into the sill of the open window. In a whirlwind pirouette, Lois brought the blue dagger around full circle and drove it deep into Hal's throat.

She ripped it out. Hal's hands flew up to the wound. He tottered backward. A stream of deep red pumped through his fingers. His eyes bulged, and his head thrust back and forth on his neck in chicken-like jerks as he gasped for air. He worked his mouth to draw a breath and made raspy gurgling noises, the stain on his sweatshirt blooming larger. He dropped to his knees and stared at her and—even while choking—Hal's hateful scowl reemerged and flushed a bright scarlet, still hard as iron, eyes burning with wrath. He tried to say something, his mug twisting as he uttered some final dying curse, but the words left his lips as nothing but a weak, waning croak.

Lois glared back at him with stunned silence, wondering *Why, Hal? What the hell happened?*

But she had no strength to ask.

His hands dropped to show a bleeding hole next to his Adam's apple that hissed with sputtering air. Hal toppled forward and went very still.

"Freeze! Police!" someone behind her demanded.

But Lois had to find her children.

"Where are my kids?" she asked without so much as meeting the eyes of the officer.

Lois crossed the granny knot with the broken toothbrush, clenched one end of the cloth in her teeth, and tied a second granny knot over the handle. Then she twisted the toothbrush to tighten the tourniquet.

"Do you live here, ma'am?" The question came after a moment of quiet as the young male cop standing at the doorway watched her apply the triage.

"Yes, I live here. I called 911. The man on the floor tried to kill me."

She climbed over the hamper, pushed through the ruined door and brushed past the cop without further thought. Two more officers lingered on the stairwell, and she passed them without a glance.

"Ma'am, you need serious medical help."

Outside, police and ambulances had arrived in droves. All the neighbors had spilled from their homes to observe the commotion. A body lay on a gurney beneath a sheet. Poor Mr. Farmer.

"Mommy!"

Maya's voice reached her through all the static of terror and shock. She came jogging up with Polly in her arms, and they both crashed into her.

"Are you okay, Mommy?!" Maya asked. "You're hurt! *Your arm!*"

Paramedics circled her like birds of prey, anxious to do their duty, but Lois didn't want to see a medic yet. She needed to be a parent. She needed to calm her children.

"Everything's okay, honey," Lois lied to them. "Everything will be fine." She'd lost her hand, her friend had been butchered, and neither her home, nor anywhere else, might ever feel safe again. This nightmare hadn't happened at the hands of some boogeyman or even a stranger, but from Hal Clement, a longtime friend and a man Lois had taught her daughters to trust.

And Lois had no explanation for any of it.

The only thing she knew with unwavering certainty was that *no*, things were *not* okay, and things would not be okay for a very long time. But to make Maya feel better, she repeated the lie to her anyway, because that's the sort of thing that a good parent does.

"Everything is going to be okay."

Jacob Mosley's Raw Deal

Six months ago...

"This place has always had a strong appetite for death." The old man's words drifted on the October breeze like fallen leaves and gave Jacob Mosley a chill.

Standing ten feet away from the park bench where the man sat, Jacob glanced around to make sure they were alone. Ducks swam on the pond, a few pigeons pecked at the grass, but no one else was in sight.

"I don't mean the pond in particular," the man continued while gazing over the murky water in front of them. He sat with his legs crossed, wearing blue coveralls and holding a wooden cane across his knees. "I mean the town. Trapper Valley. Shady Brake. The surrounding areas. This whole countryside has always been hungrier for it than most places. Long as I can remember."

"You're Mr. Nix?"

The man turned to him with searching eyes and an ashen face. Jacob guessed him to be in his seventies, at least, based on the thin white hair and drooping eyelids.

"I am Christopher Nix. What you might call the unofficial historian of the town. One of them, anyway. I presume you are Mr. Mosley."

"Yes, sir." Jacob approached and offered his hand. Nix shook it weakly. "I'm Jacob Mosley. Pleased to meet you."

"Mmm," he said, looking Jacob over. "When someone contacts me regarding local lore instead of consulting the esteemed owner of our local book shop, it usually means the stranger is looking for information that's not found in a book."

"I'm no stranger," Jacob said. "Lived here all my life. Starting pitcher for the Trapper Valley Wildcats for three seasons. We won county a couple years ago."

Mr. Nix's expression remained blank and unreadable. "Sorry. I don't follow baseball." He turned back to the pond. "But congratulations on your success."

"I already tried Mr. Burnside at the bookstore. He couldn't help me. He gave your phone number."

Mr. Nix stared at the shifting colors of the pond, its surface rippling a fractured reflection of the tall pines and morning sky. Jacob found the glimmering light almost hypnotic.

"If Mr. Burnside sent you to me, then he must not feel comfortable with your field of inquiry."

"That's the impression I got. You mind if I sit?"

"Burnside is a nervous man. He has shared the secrets of this place in the past, and people have suffered dearly as a result."

"Really? How's that?" Jacob took a seat beside Mr. Nix on the wood slats where the green paint was chipped and peeling.

"He passed along information. Others misused that information."

A young woman jogged through the park in tights and a T-shirt. She waved as she passed the bench.

"Why is that his fault?" Jacob said.

"It isn't. But he doesn't want it to happen again."

"But you're willing to tell me what he wouldn't?"

Mr. Nix slowly turned to him, his eyes dark and deep. "Burnside wants a clear conscience. He feels the need to protect people from themselves. I, on the other hand, think the world has a population problem."

The way Nix held his gaze, hard and implacable without a shred of humor, told Jacob to watch himself. This old man might be a snake.

"That's not a very neighborly sentiment."

"You aren't my neighbor," Nix said.

Jacob turned to the water, and the shimmering ripples eased his ire at the man. "Look, I don't mean any harm. I don't want a magical path to fame and fortune, or anything like that. Truth is, I'm sick. Malignant tumor. Got a matter of months, tops. Doctors can't do a thing at this point." He turned back to the man's bloodless stare, which had never faltered. "Truth is, Mr. Nix ... I don't want to die. And that's exactly what's going to happen to me, short of a miracle."

Mr. Nix watched two ducks glide down and skid onto the water. "That's why you tracked me down?"

"Yes, sir. That is the reason why. I'm in search of a miracle."

Mr. Nix fixed his gaze on the pond for a long stretch without saying a word. Jacob let him weigh the request in peace.

"How old are you, son?"

"Twenty."

Nix gave a long sigh, which seemed to deflate his upper body. Then he shook his head. "Twenty... Too young to get sick like you are. And just stupid enough to pursue what you're pursuing." He looked at Jacob. "There is a high cost, of course. For what you want, there's always a price and it often outweighs the gains you seek in the first place. See? It's a trick. Always. A cosmic sleight of hand. Nobody who toys around with hill magic ever comes out on top. Oh, I'm sure you've heard stories to the contrary, but they're all lies. People have used it and prospered, sure, but they're always hiding something insidious, some sick, black price they had to pay for their good fortune. It's impossible to know the price for the magic until it's too late, and you're already damned to hell. Don't you understand?"

"I understand what you're saying," Jacob said. "But you need to understand this: I don't believe in hell. Or heaven, either. That's why I don't want to die. And I'm willing to try anything."

Nix gazed back at the pond and nodded. "So be it."

***

Now...

Jacob waved for the bartender at the Rusty Hinge. "Another round for me and my friends, please."

The bartender grabbed three clean highball glasses, clinked ice into each, then filled all three with two fingers of bourbon. He sloshed the drinks onto a tray and walked them over to the small round table where Jacob sat with the Johnson brothers, Angus and Lemmy.

"Here ya go." The bartender placed the drinks on the table. "Three fire-waters. I'll add them to your tab."

"Much obliged," Jacob said.

Angus wrapped his stubby fingers around a glass and lifted it in front of his ruddy face. "Here's to your health, Jake. We thank you kindly for the drinks."

"Here's to you, kid," the larger brother added, raising his drink and tilting it into his bushy black beard.

Jacob took a belt of the booze and wiped his lips. "Least I could do is buy a man a drink after he gets out of the joint."

Lemmy shook his head and blew through his nose. "It was tough in there. Boring."

Jacob laughed. "*Boring* ... Listen to you. You're a neck-breaker, that's the only reason you found it boring. Shit. Skinny boy like me goes up the creek, I don't think I'd find it *boring*."

Lemmy's hairy face opened to reveal a big yellow grin. His laugh was an old combustion engine rolling over. "No. You'd be fighting off the butt-pirates. Least I *hope* you'd be fighting em off."

Angus added to the laughter. "So tell me, kid. How'd a young fella like you come into enough money wheres you can buy all these whiskeys for me and my jail-bird brother?"

Jacob peered up from his drink and flashed them a smile. "Learned from you guys. Watched how you did things and started something of my own."

The Johnsons looked at each other then back at Jacob, and the humor faded from Angus' face. "Started something, huh? I hope you don't mean what I think you mean. 'Cause we set up shop here a long time ago. We got business interests and we ain't big on sharing. Are we, Lemmy?"

"No, we ain't," his brother grumbled.

"Calm down. I don't operate around here. I'm selling over the mountain to all the rich kids. I know y'all got the Valley and the Brake. You think I'm crazy? Gonna get you drunk just to piss you off?"

They glanced at each other again. Angus finished his drink. "Okay, then. What's your angle? My brother gets sprung free, and you show back in town on the very same night. You running into us here was no accident."

"You got me," Jacob said, raising his palms in a gesture of surrender. "I got word Lemmy was getting out today. Figured y'all'd be headed to the bar, putting your heads together, getting business back on track. I wanted to come by, say hello, and maybe talk business with you."

"What kind of business?" Lemmy asked through his Viking beard.

"Big business. For both of us. I'm talking about supplying your product, so you don't have to fuck with the Mexicans anymore. I'm talking the highest quality primo coke you can find and provided to you at a bargain-basement price, compared to what you're currently paying your Latino friends. You can leave meth to the lowlifes and stick to the good stuff, and deal only with the best—and wealthiest—clientele around."

For a moment they only stared at him. Angus leaned over to his brother and mumbled something in his ear, then returned to Jacob with a suspicious scowl. "Me and my brother need a minute to discuss this proposal in private."

Jacob nodded. "Absolutely. Take some time. Chew it over. I'll be at the bar, refilling my beverage."

He ordered another round and sipped his drink from a barstool. He could not make out what the brothers were saying over the sports commentators on TV prattling about football.

Eventually Angus waved him back over to the table. "We decided we need to see for ourselves the quality and quantity of merchandise you're talkin' about."

Jacob jingled the melting ice cubes in his glass then tipped it back to drain the last drops of liquid. "I figured you'd say something like that. If you've had your fill of whiskey, then follow me. I've got something to show you."

***

Roy Ford sat alone in a dark corner of the bar sporting shaggy hair, a new Fu Manchu, and a U. of Alabama baseball hat pulled down low over his eyes. He sucked on a cigarette and sipped at a Budweiser. He didn't look like a sheriff's deputy, and that was the idea. He was off-duty. This was a personal call regarding two very predictable brothers who had never been worth spit. One of them had just been freed upon the world without having paid a suitable penance for his past sins, and Roy planned to correct that great injustice. Tonight.

He'd not expected to see the Mosley kid with them. Roy hadn't seen Jacob around town since the kid's baseball days. He'd heard a rumor that Jacob had taken ill, but had hoped the gossip was bunk and that the kid had actually landed a scholarship, moved away and tried to make something of himself. Not everyone had the talent to get out of this shitburg, but that boy had shown promise with a fastball the speed of sound. Now he sat with two well-known scumbags in the local dive and appeared to be scheming with them. So much for making something of himself.

Roy turned his chair to the football game as Jacob and the men stood to leave. He'd changed his appearance but knew a man's eyes could give away secrets, so he kept them averted.

When they walked out the door, Roy laid five dollars on the bar and followed them at a cautious distance.

***

Jacob Mosley pulled his car up to a lakeside trailer in the country twenty-some miles outside Shady Brake. Next to its front door, a single bulb, mounted to the wall in a glass jar, offered the only light aside from the approaching headlamps. The Johnson brothers pulled up the gravel road and parked their truck alongside him. They killed the engine, leaving only the hum of a nearby generator and the buzz of a zillion crickets. The high-beams went dim, making the corrugated gray shack look eerily lonesome all by itself.

Jacob climbed the detached three-tread stairs that lead to the entry. He slid his key into the deadbolt and signaled the Johnsons with a jerk of his head. "Come on, it's cool. We're alone."

Angus stood outside the truck. "Alone? You got what you claim you got, and you leave it out here unguarded?"

Jacob opened the trailer door and flipped a switch on the wall. The interior came to life with a bright glow. He backed off the steps into the grass. "Not much to guard. Only a little left around here. I keep most of the product stored in town. It's a lot more convenient when I need it."

"In town?" Lemmy said as both brothers walked up to the trailer. "So why we here?"

"I wanted you to see the operation. Show you how the sausage gets made." He gestured to the door. "After you gentlemen."

The brothers looked at one another. Then Lemmy took a heavy breath and lurched up the steps. Angus followed. As they stepped inside, their footsteps made a rustling noise on the floor.

"What's with all the plastic sheeting?" Lemmy asked.

Jacob said, "It's all part of the process."

From behind he jammed a syringe into each of their necks. They growled as he sunk the plungers and shoved them both forward. Angus spilled onto the sheeted floor, but Lemmy stayed upright. He whirled around and lunged for Jacob, who sprang back out the door. Stumbling, but regaining his stride, Jacob shot around the corner of the building.

Gunfire rang out behind him.

"What the hell did you stick us with?!" Angus yelled from inside.

Reaching the rear of the trailer and sprinting for a thicket of trees, Jacob cast a glance back as Lemmy rounded the corner firing a pistol.

Lemmy shouted something at him, but the words slurred together unintelligibly. He shouted again, and his voice slowed down and stretched out like a song played on the wrong speed. Jacob looked back again to see the big man stagger and then fall face-first to the ground. Angus' cursing from inside had gone quiet too.

Jacob stopped running and dropped his hands to his knees. He snatched huge gasps of air, stood up then doubled back. He stuck Lemmy's pistol into his own waistband, then lifted the oaf beneath the armpits and dragged him back to the trailer.

***

When the trailer came into view, Roy Ford hit the brakes of his Chevy. The wooded road opened into a barren lot where rocky ground choked off most of the overgrowth. That's where the two vehicles ahead of him had stopped driving.

Navigating the stony path without headlights had been a chore, and Roy's biggest fear had been getting his pickup stuck in a trench along the way. Now, as he idled inside the darkened mouth of the road, he worried he'd be discovered before he was ready to make his move. First he wanted a closer look at exactly what these men were up to.

Roy checked the clip of his Ruger nine-millimeter: ten rounds, fully loaded. A second clip hung on his belt. He put on gloves and slipped on a black ski mask, leaving only his eyes exposed. He zipped up his navy blue jacket, carefully opened the driver's door and crept outside. He stalked along the clearing's perimeter, keeping near the trees should he need to slip inside for cover until he got past the glow of the front light.

Once cast in shadow, he darted to end of the trailer, knelt down and pressed his ear to the siding. The hum of a generator. The ecstatic buzz of every cricket within miles. A thump and a shuffle from inside the shack, but Roy could make out no voices.

The trailer stood off the ground on block piers with no underpinning to skirt its edges. Roy dropped low and crawled underneath on hands and knees, listening for even the slightest human voice. Tonight's mission might be unofficial, but tomorrow would be different, and if he could unravel a new criminal plot in the process, then all the better for him and all the worse for the Johnsons.

But Roy caught neither a word nor a whisper—and that was odd for three scoundrels hiding in the sticks. A paranoid dread seeped in from the darkness as he considered their silence could mean he'd already been spotted, and they were devising a plan to deal with him.

But that didn't sit right either, as all the stomping and clomping and banging around the floor above him meant they were engaged in some sort of activity where silence wasn't of particular concern. And although he heard no words, there was an occasional grunt and gasp, which had him at a loss—surely they weren't involved in some sort of *gay* thing.

He had to have a look. The windows were too high, the only one in reach being the small diamond-shaped pane in the front door. That's the direction he crept, prowling like a cat. He paused at the steps and reached out with his ears only to find the incessant crickets and hum of the generator, but nothing else. Even the thumping and bumping had waned. With careful balance and a cautious stride, he scaled the three steps and peered into the window.

Jacob Mosley looked back at him from where he stood over Angus Johnson, whose gaping neck streamed dark blood into a glass that Jacob held.

Roy's heart skipped a beat.

A surge of surprise passed over Jacob's face on being discovered. But he lifted the dripping glass and tilted it back undeterred, swallowing the syrup in thick gulps, which made Roy's stomach turn.

Roy shook away a faint spell, hardened his core and gripped the doorknob. Not even locked; he slung it open and burst into the trailer, gun drawn.

"County sheriff! Don't you move!" He swept the room with the pistol.

Jacob set the tall glass on the kitchen table next to the very dead Angus Johnson. He wiped his hands on his gory shirt. "Look, let me explain," he told Roy, "I know this looks bad."

The floor was covered in thick translucent sheeting that bunched up against the trailer walls. Puddles formed from what leaked out of Angus.

"You're under arrest! Hands above your head!"

"Sheriffs don't wear ski masks."

That piece-of-shit Lemmy Johnson lay facedown and motionless next to a wall, that same face partially obscured in plastic.

"He dead, too?"

"Not yet," Jacob said. "He's just—"

"What the hell is this? Some kind of slaughterhouse? Jesus Christ, this is ungodly."

"Roy?" Jacob wiped his mouth with his sleeve. "Roy Ford? That you?"

Roy lifted his nine to head level. "Don't come any closer."

"What's with the mask, Roy?"

Roy peeled back the mask and let it cling to his scalp. The air cooled his face, and breathing came easier. "I'm taking you in.'"

Jacob hung his head. "First, I really need you to hear me out."

"I'm taking Lemmy in, too."

"No, Roy, you're going to let me have him. That's why you're out here tonight, right? To take out the trash? To kill the drunk who ran over Maysie? Your daughter...?"

"Don't you talk about her." The sound of her name stabbed Roy in the gut.

"Look, I get it. I understand completely, and I'm in a position to help you. And now it seems that you're in a position to help me. All you gotta do is walk away. Let me take care of this mess. I'll take out the trash for you." He talked with his hands, making little chops in the air.

"No." Roy found his throat dry. "I can't be a part of whatever this is. It ain't holy."

"Well, you're right about that," Jacob said with a thin, exasperated laugh, blood dripping from his chin. "It ain't holy. But neither is vengeance, Roy. I do believe your God says something about that in the bible. Vengeance is His; not yours. Right? So why don't you just turn around and let me get on with doing the Lord's work."

"Might as well add blasphemy to the reasons you'll burn. You're already a murderer."

"Hell, I didn't realize you were so damn religious, Roy. You sound like a regular bible-thumper these days."

"That's 'cause I ain't ever seen anything so devilish."

Jacob placed his index fingers against his temples. He closed his eyes and bowed his head. "Just go away, Roy. You're in the wrong place at the wrong time. You'll be making a grave mistake if you don't just go away."

Roy stared at the unconscious Lemmy with a raging hatred and silently begged God for permission to focus his aim and blow out the bastard's brains. But this bloodbath with the Mosley kid had shaken his moorings, and he wasn't thinking straight. This had become a sticky situation; make the wrong move, and he could go down for murder, just like the kid.

He gestured the gun at Lemmy and told Jacob, "You pick him up, drag him outside."

"Look, Roy, just—"

"*Shut up*! No more talking. Do what I say or I'll put a bullet in you."

"I really wish you wouldn't."

Roy fired a shot to the left of Jacob, and glass burst from a window behind him.

"I said move."

Jacob moved.

***

Forced into the sheriff's station with a gun at his back, Jacob's heart dropped at the sight of the girl at the dispatcher's desk. There sat Jody Sutton of all people, with her curly red hair and freckles, those bright eyes and always cheerful smile. Like a flower in the mud, she'd always stood out from the crowd as they'd grown up together—not because she was especially pretty, but because she radiated a sunny happiness that infected those around her, even wise-guys like himself.

This was the last place he wanted to see her. Must be a new job.

"Jacob?!" she gasped, drawing a hand to her mouth, her thin eyebrows lifting in an arch. She dropped the paperback she'd been reading and rose from her chair, revealing the big round belly of an expectant mother. "Oh gosh, are you hurt?"

"Stay back, Jody," Roy ordered from behind him. "I have him in custody for murder."

Her eyes and mouth shrank at mention of the word.

"It's a misunderstanding," Jacob said.

"Hell it is!" Roy pushed him toward a holding cell at the end of the room. "Caught him red-handed. And you wouldn't believe what else I saw him doing."

"Don't listen to him, Jody."

Jody looked perfectly confused, swiveling her head between two men she'd known for years.

"Angus Johnson is dead out in the woods past Crenshaw Hollow. His brother is cuffed in my Jeep outside. Out cold. Drugged up."

"I thought you were off tonight, Roy," Jody said softly.

"I was. Where's Dawson?" Roy shoved Jacob into the cell doorway and clanged the barred door closed.

"Out on patrol."

"Get him on the radio."

"Listen to me, Jody," Jacob said through the black metal bars. "Don't listen to this asshole. He's in more danger than he can comprehend. But you've always been smart. So listen: Let me out of here. *Let me out*. I'm running out of time."

"Jody, call Dawson." Roy unzipped his coat and hung it on a rack.

"What are you naming the baby, Jody?" Jacob asked.

She blinked twice then looked down and patted her tummy. "Um, Nathan … It's a boy … Naming him after my daddy."

"Nathan. That's a fine name. Now Jody, for your sake and that of Nathan there, I need you to get the keys to this cell and let me go. Tonight's the full moon. If I don't get done what I've got to do before the moon wanes, then everyone around me is going to die. You. Roy. Nathan, too."

She recoiled at that, and Jacob worried she might lose all regard for him and tune him out.

"Don't listen to him," Roy said. "He's been spouting this crazy shit since I picked him up. I saw him drinking blood right out of Angus' neck. He'd cut him wide open."

Jody pressed a hand to her forehead.

"I'm not threatening you, Jody," Jacob said to her. "Please understand. I'm trying to warn you. I'm trying to save you. The truth will sound bizarre, but I had to kill Angus Johnson because he was an evil man. And Lemmy, he's evil too. He's as rotten as they come. Right, Roy?"

Roy's chin sunk. His expression darkened.

Jacob continued, "That's right. Lemmy: In a blind stupor he barreled his shitty old truck down Grayson Drive right into your little girl. Drove right over the poor thing, bicycle and all. Doesn't a man like that deserve to die, Roy? I know you believe that."

"Just shut up," Roy said with a hitch in his voice and water in his eyes.

"And you've got to let me do it, Roy. Because I'm caught up in some hill-magic shit that won't make any sense to anyone who's never experienced it."

"You've lost your ever-lovin' mind."

"It's all about sacrifices, Roy. Remember how I was sick? That tumor? Well, I've got something else inside me now. Something different. Something very, very old. I have to keep it happy with sacrifices every lunar cycle. So I look for black-hearted people who deserve what they've got coming. Because if I don't drink the dying blood of a third and final human before the moon falls tonight, then what's inside me will come out again, and it doesn't discriminate between what type of people it feeds on."

"Bullshit."

As his patience for Roy Ford evaporated, Jacob turned to Jody, whose pursed lips and saddened eyes showed genuine concern—but Jacob recognized it was concern for his mental state and not for her own life, nor that of her child.

"If we had any time, I'd tell you to look up Old Man Nix. He got me into this. Maybe he'll tell you what he told me. Then again, maybe you shouldn't hear it. Because you go down some paths, and there's no turning back."

"Mr. Nix?" Jody said. "Why are you wrapped up with that old creep?"

"Self-preservation," he said. "But it came with a price. That's what I was trying to pay when super-trooper here showed up to save the day."

"Tell it to the judge." Roy walked out the double doors of the station.

"Shit!" Jacob spat. "No time, no time, no time ... You've got to believe me, Jody ... Germantown. *Germantown*! Germantown, Tennessee! Does that ring a bell?"

Jacob fixed an iron gaze on her, trying to speak with his eyes, trying to establish a connection to an old friend and surpass her better judgement.

"Germantown ... Sounds familiar," she said.

"Of course it does. Story made big national headlines. Germantown—a wealthy suburb of Memphis. Remember the murders? The massacre? All those bodies torn apart at a country club, strewn over a golf course. A bunch of houses burned?"

"I think so."

Jacob tapped himself in the chest.

"What are you saying?" Jody asked.

"I was there."

"So?"

"So ... I didn't get the job done. Some fat-cat rapist weaseled out of a child-molestation rap because he had money and the kid's parents didn't. I had him marked for Number Three. But security guards showed up. Things went haywire. What can I say ... I'm new at this."

"I'm not following you."

"I didn't make the third sacrifice. I ran out of time, so everybody died—the good, the bad and the ugly. See, when the moon disappears, that's when things change. I have no control anymore, and nothing will be able to stop what's coming."

The station doors banged open and Roy backed into the lobby with Lemmy Johnson's gorilla arms dangling from the crooks of his elbows. Sheriff Dawson Andrews followed inside carrying the body by the ankles. Lemmy's head lolled backwards, and he snored from the large brown hole in his beard. They neared the holding cell across from Jacob's in the adjacent corner of the building. At the door, Roy straightened his arms and dropped Lemmy. His head smacked the floor with a whap.

"Woops." Roy fished the keys from his pocket and unlocked the cell, stuffing Lemmy inside.

"The moon," Jacob said to the officers. "Where's the moon? Still high in the sky?"

"What is he talking about?" Dawson asked. He stood taller than six feet with a flabby belly, a pie-shaped face, and the bushy mustache of cops and firemen.

"He's lost it," Roy muttered.

"The moon," Jacob persisted. "Because I'm feeling kind of funny. Is it high in the sky or ready to set?"

"Sunrise ain't 'til a couple hours," Dawson said, looking Jacob up and down. "Nothing you need to worry about."

"It's not the sunrise that worries me. It's when the moon falls."

"That right? Well, I hate to disappoint you, hotshot, but I didn't see much of a moon out there. I reckon she's sinkin' behind the clouds about now."

Jacob's breathing grew heavy and labored. His blood flowed hotly though his veins. The internal throbbing he'd experienced once before—back in Germantown—pestered him with a recurrent cry of faint human voices, an ethereal sound which transcended his ears, like a chorus of pleas from a choir of ghostly children.

The strength in his legs melted away. He folded to his knees and moaned, "Oh no. Please, please no."

"Wow." Dawson strolled across the lobby and poured himself a coffee from the office carafe. "You really got a live one here, Ford."

"And I wasn't even supposed to be here today," Roy said as he sat in his computer chair. He lifted his legs and rested his boots on the desk.

"Jody," Jacob said, conscious of the strange echoing resonance now in his voice which originated from somewhere that wasn't here. "Jody, listen to me. It's too late to convince these two. You have to run. You have to run, now. For the love of your baby, if nothing else. Drop everything and run to your car. Run for your fucking life. Drive away as fast and as far as you can."

Jody hovered above her desk chair, wringing her hands. She looked to the men for guidance. The officers only scoffed at him, but her trembling lip and whitened pallor told Jacob he was getting through to her.

"You're scaring me, Jacob," she said.

The veins on his arms swelled into jungle vines. Sweat poured down his face. Pressure built in his head like a pneumatic tank inside his skull, pushing outward in every direction.

"Scaring you?" Jacob said in a ragged voice that he could barely make out himself. "I'm going to split you wide open and rip your soft-boiled baby right out of you, placenta and all."

The words knocked her back a step. Her face went slack and her arms quaked.

"I'm going to stuff little Nathan's corpse in your mouth, Jody, and make you swallow it down. I'm going to tear off Roy's head and shove it up the ass of his fat partner there. Then me and Lemmy Johnson are gonna piss all over both of them, because Lemmy's a fucking standup guy. Right, Roy? 'Cause he likes killing too, and hell I warned you but *it's too fucking late!*"

Jody bolted for the doors. She slung one open with a bang and darted outside, wailing as she fled.

"You sick sonofabitch!" Dawson said. He approached Jacob's cell with his hand on his taser. "Shut the fuck up or I'll light you up right in your cage."

Roy shot out of the station chasing Jody.

Jacob quivered in a mound, racked by a ravenous hunger and a disintegrating sense of self control. He peered up and locked eyes with the sheriff. Jacob rose to his feet with the low quaking growl of a beast. Somewhere deep within him, the last vestiges of his humanity gave a final, ominous snap and broke away.

***

"Jody! Come on back here!" Roy shouted as she climbed into her Mazda at the far side of the parking lot. "The guy's gone crazy! Don't listen to that garbage!"

The slammed door made it clear where she stood on the matter. She fired the car backward, swerved around with a chirp of the tires, and shot down the road.

Roy shook his head and wandered back to the station. Jacob Mosley needed to shut his crazy trap, and if he refused, then maybe fifty-thousand volts from a taser would help persuade him. Hell, Dawson might have already given him the juice himself.

On the way inside he cast a glance at the sky. Dawn would break soon. He saw no moon, only deep night.

Roy didn't see his fellow officer on entering the station. No one sat at dispatch, no one in the partitioned corner office, no one at the deputy's desk or in the two lobby chairs. The bathroom door to his left hung ajar to a darkened interior.

The holding cells were walled in cinderblock and occupied the two far corners of the building, with opposing doors that had a short access hallway between them. From his current angle Roy had no view inside the walled cells, but the broken bars of the last one on the left—Jacob Mosley's quarters—bent outward at extreme angles. A wet swath of dark liquid trailed from the cell to a wide puddle in the middle of the hall, where the overhead fluorescents reflected crimson.

"Dawson?" Roy said. The hair follicles prickled across the back of his neck. "Dawson? Mosley?"

Instead of an answer, a scratching and squelching noise came from the cell, a wet, rough sound like footsteps trudging through mud. Roy drew his sidearm. He took a cautious stride forward with slow steady breaths to remain calm.

"Whoever's in that cell, identify yourself! I am an armed police officer. Identify yourself! Mosley, that you?"

Only the noise replied, growing louder with proximity. The moist smacking brought to mind Roy's pet Basset Hound, Elmo, at feeding time, when the dog would lap and chew greedily at the Gravy Train Roy would prepare with warm water.

Nothing good or righteous was in that cell, so Roy summoned every ounce of courage and even thought a silent prayer—a *guilty* prayer coupled with a plea for forgiveness, since he'd nearly strayed and killed a man. And even though he still believed deeply that Lemmy Johnson deserved a bullet in the gut, Roy had come to terms with the notion that it wasn't his place to enforce such a judgement. He'd made that determination based on the wickedness unfolding before his eyes, because this much blood spilled in this tiny station could only be explained by something evil, which meant God was angry and had turned away.

"Dawson?" As he moved down the hall he gained an obscured view into the cell doors. The red carpet of blood thickened as it led into Jacob Mosley's cell, but he could not yet see anyone inside, nor could he see Lemmy in the cell across the hall. "Dawson, if you can hear me, please respond."

No answer.

Roy lifted his mobile and phoned another off-duty deputy. He got no answer. He then dialed the Trapper Valley Police Department nearby to request emergency backup. They assured him officers were on the way.

He pressed his back against the block wall of Mosley's cell and slid toward the door. Sweat from his palm dripped down the pistol grip and tickled his wrist. From his new position, he gained a better view inside Lemmy's cell, but the big man no longer lay in a heap against the wall where he and Dawson had left him.

"Johnson!" Roy called out. "Lemmy Johnson, can you hear me?"

With a clang, Lemmy slammed into the barred door and stayed there, face pressed against the metal, eyes half-open and bloodshot. He struggled in place with his arms pulled behind in cuffs, as though something invisible held him fast. Roy aimed his nine into the cell, but nothing else appeared. No target to shoot at but Lemmy alone, who groaned and shook as the metal rattled against him.

"What'sssss happenin' to meeee?" Lemmy groaned. His beard opened with a scream as he was pressed into the door. With a wet crunch the steel bars sunk into his face and ribs, shoulders and thighs—*snickety-snap!* His skull and torso slid like ground meat through the grate, cleaving bone and flesh. Thick, butchered slabs of Lemmy sloughed through the openings and toppled down into the hallway.

Roy leapt away from the splash. He spouted a string of curses, but no words escaped. His voice had abandoned his mouth, dry as a desert. He tore his gaze away from the gut-wrenching butchery, his eyes shut tight to drive the gray from his vision, so as to not pass out.

"Lemmy's dead now," said a soft familiar voice from Mosley's jail cell on Roy's left. "I'll bet seeing it happen felt really good. Right, Dad?"

Dear God in heaven… He knew that voice like it was his own, because in a way, it had once been his own. It was his daughter's voice.

Roy leveled the gun before him and turned to face the entry, both hoping and dreading. The chewing noise met his ears again. His throat tightened as he neared the ruined door. Inside the cell, the lake of blood spread nearly to the walls. Sheriff Dawson's lifeless face gawked at the ceiling from the puddle on the cell floor.

Ice coursed through Roy, and his grip tightened on the gun with cramping force. Dawson's face was his only recognizable feature. Obliterated, his body lay flayed open on its back, everything nature had stuffed him with spilled, slit to the bone along each limb and split wide from his groin to his grin. Only powered machinery could have achieved such ghastly results, but no tools lay in the cell. Instead, a small figure with thin hands crouched over the red pile of muscle and organs. She worked her fingers deep into the soft tissues, pulling free what she wanted, and brought little handfuls to her mouth. She ate with a suckling sound.

"M … M… Maysie?" Roy said.

Those big brown eyes peered up and liquefied him. It was her; it had to be her, because the Lord only made one pair of eyes that beautiful. She even wore the same green sweater as on the day of the accident. But Roy's mind reeled with the concrete knowledge that what he saw simply could not be.

"What'd you expect?" she asked in that voice he'd so longed to hear again. "Horns and a pitchfork?" She giggled her signature laugh, always light and airy, a whimsical chime that had warmed his soul and echoed within him ever since he'd last seen her alive. She flashed a ruby smile. It dripped.

"Oh, honey," Roy said, voice parched and hoarse. The warmth of tears touched his cheeks. "Oh honey, I love you. I love you so much, but this ... this can't really be you." But that chocolate brown hair, that cute pug nose, those two unmistakable dimples tugged at his heart.

Maysie's eyes, sparkling as ever, squinted as she laughed again. But that laugh changed its timbre as it sank into something distant, something low and malevolent. "Of course I'm not your daughter. She's dead but she's conscious, and will be forever burning in the fires of hell. Her flesh blisters and blackens then falls off like bark, over and over again, all while she screams for her daddy."

Rage swept over Roy in a wave of flame. He aimed ready to fire, to end the evil in one brash instant, but couldn't or maybe wouldn't. Pulling that trigger was out of the question. To harm his sweet child, bloodthirsty or not, would be a fate worse than death. So Roy froze with his daughter's smile in his gun sights.

The wail of police sirens grew in the distance.

He focused on the impostor's gleaming brown eyes and asked, "Just what in God's name are you?"

"Nos sunt in predonum," she spoke in Maysie's six-year-old falsetto. "Somos los depredadores," she then said in an ethereal baritone that echoed from some other faraway place. "We are here to eat you."

Roy shot a glance behind him and saw only slices of Lemmy. He scanned left and right.

"Who is 'we'?"

The gun flew from Roy's hand and clattered across the linoleum. He floated off his feet. He kicked and found no floor. His arms snapped straight backward, like he had a foot on his back and someone behind him was trying to tear them off. With a loud crack, his shoulder joints popped from their sockets, prying even further behind him and constricting his chest. Breath poured out of his lungs. There he hovered, helpless.

"Say your prayers, law-man." The Maysie-thing's smile widened. She'd been missing two front teeth on the bottom row, but her little face now wielded a mouthful of pointed incisors which elongated and multiplied as those lips stretched and expanded.

"Oh, honey," Roy said as the shape of her head swelled and flexed to contain her widening jaws and all the dagger-like teeth. She gained height as her head grew, warped and mutated into a giant gaping maw. Roy's vision collapsed and centered on the deep, black tunnel which led down his precious daughter's abyss of a throat. He found himself helpless to resist as all those sharp, drooling points drew so very close.

At last, Roy saw only darkness and teeth, and heard the words: "Freeze! Trapper Valley Police!"

***

Thunder rippled from an angry horizon as Jacob Mosley hiked across a small hill covered in cropped dead grass. The slope led down to a broad pond where an old man sat on a park bench and watched the water. The man had his back turned. As Jacob approached, he slipped a hand into his black leather jacket, nerves buzzing and sparking. Inside the pocket, Jacob kept a switchblade, always razor sharp, as well as a pack of Marlboros, which he pulled out and packed with his palm.

He took a seat next to Mr. Nix. "Looks like it might rain," Jacob offered as a means of greeting him. He lit a cigarette, took a drag and released a plume of smoke.

Nix's gray eyes crawled over him. Today the old man wore a green baseball hat from the local Burger Hut, but his face remained as implacable as ever. "Reckon it might," he said as his gaze returned to the sparkling pond.

Maybe the old man saw some great truth in the pond, so Jacob studied it too.

"All the dead police officers," Nix said. "That your handiwork?"

Jacob took a deep breath and exhaled through his nose. He thought for a moment. "I have no recollection of doing anything like that. But I probably am responsible."

Nix shook his head. "A wicked shame. Some fine men lost their lives. Fathers. Brothers. Sons. Not the type who deserve it."

"I didn't intend for things to turn out the way they did. I never wanted this. When I was sick I just didn't want to die. Now ... all I want to do is die. And it seems I can't."

Nix looked down and slowly traced a long finger along the mahogany cane across his knees. "This place has always had a strong appetite for death." He turned to Jacob. "Is that why you're here? To kill me? For telling you what I told you? For pointing you to the hills?"

Jacob puffed on his Marlboro and focused on the coal as it glowed hot. Then he let it die and blew a cloud of smoke.

"I don't blame you," Jacob said. "I blame myself."

Upon hearing this, Nix slowly nodded and turned back to the pond. "I must say that I'm relieved to hear that. You see, son, I do empathize with your predicament. Free will: She can be a real bitch. I guess some fellows are hard-headed. You and me both. We're destined to learn our lessons the hard way."

A fat brown toad hopped from beneath their bench and took two jumps toward the pond, landing next to Jacob's foot. Nix's tongue shot out of his mouth like a thick pink rope and snatched the toad off the ground. He slurped it through the air and back between his teeth. The old man's cheeks plumped and wriggled as he chewed it up, gorging the whole thing at once with a moist smacking noise. A last dangling leg disappeared between his lips as a drop of brown juice dribbled down his chin. Then he turned back to the pond.

After a long, frozen moment, Jacob unclenched his jaw and regained his breath. He gazed back at the pond along with Nix, who he suddenly understood with greater measure. No wonder the old man liked looking at the pond. As its surface rippled, the water reflected the natural world around them in countless fragmented images, in little bits and pieces.

Story Notes

Suburban Facebreaker is nasty little number inspired by the prevailing late-70s house design in the neighborhood where I lived and wrote the story. Many of the homes were built with concrete steps, of which I became particularly wary once I had kids who needed help climbing them. I was afraid one of my sons might miss a step, tumble down a full flight of those hard, sharp angles, and hurt themselves terribly. I packaged that fear into a plot device where a character deliberately sets a trap to make such a fall happen. But what kind of character would do such a thing? Probably someone who felt entirely justified in their actions, that's who. I conjured up the protective (and vindictive) grandmother, Vivienne Reynolds, a character that should ring familiar with anyone who's ever lived in the South, where people can be just as sweet as pie, as long as you don't go messing with their family.

Silly Rabbits began as a werewolf story for a submission call to a werewolf-themed anthology, but it ended as something very different. The problem I have with traditional monsters like werewolves, vampires, zombies, etc. is that they've been covered exhaustively, and it's hard to come up with an original spin on the things. Plus, I'm a writer—a creative type—and I didn't create those traditional monsters; some other writer did. Writing about them feels like playing with someone else's toys. As I was developing the story, I decided I couldn't limit myself to werewolves, so I gave the plot a drastic left turn. I think my decision injected a lot more originality and inventiveness into the tale, even if it disqualified me from the wolf-centric anthology that inspired it.

Of All the Nights is a little different from the other tales in *Teeth Marks* because I was intentionally trying to keep the horror "off the page" and build tension around a looming threat that grows in the periphery of the story. I love fiction with blood and guts and well-drawn beasties, but I also love atmosphere, suspense and character depth. In this one, I tried to focus less on action and more on developing an encroaching sense of dread.

Burt's Top Secret Spice Mix was inspired by Sam's Super Sandwiches in Birmingham, Al. I've been eating there since I was a teenager (best hot dogs in town!). While gobbling down a Super Burger one afternoon I noticed a news clipping framed on the store wall where a local paper had interviewed Sam, the owner. A quote from him mentioned that he had trouble remembering customer names but always remembered the orders of his regulars, so their orders essentially doubled as secret nicknames he had for them. That tidbit provided my character voice for Burt (Sam's stand-in), so then I needed a plot. What kind of problems would Burt encounter in his sandwich shop? I decided a criminal extortionist would do the trick, and pitted the two against each other.

Waist Deep is a gory one originally published in *Rejected for Content 3*. Before writing, I usually need an overall framework as to how a story will unfold from beginning to end. Not this one. I opened *in media res* with a stabbing in a secluded hunting shack, and then tried to plot my way out of that opening scene. Why did these three men stab another man to death? I went for broke with a "grindhouse" style story and I'm happy with how it turned out, as gruesome as it may be.

Louise, Your Shed's on Fire is the most comedic story in the book and has been produced by *The Wicked Library* podcast as an audio drama for free streaming and download. The story is an homage to "alien invasion" movies and books, and the first-person narration of the well-meaning Meg Thatcher was a fun character to write. Listen to the story at thewickedlibrary.com.

Slice of Heaven is the tale of a stalker. I originally penned this one for an anthology call where the theme focused on stories in which a character knowingly invites something evil or threatening into their lives. But why would a "good" person welcome bad things? After stewing on the question, I decided maybe someone needed to use that "bad thing"—if only momentarily—to counter an even greater, more pressing threat at the time. That was the seed of the plot, and since I delivered pizza in the past, I thought the job would make a good "mobile" setting for plenty of stalking opportunity.

Cookies originally saw print in *Creepy Campfire Quarterly No. 4*, and I was aiming to write a dark modern fable. There's a long tradition of stories where good people—often children—treat animals (or monsters) with kindness, and then have that kindness rewarded when that animal (or monster) comes to their rescue. That's the basic framework here, but it's too familiar a story trope to be original, so I gave the plot a twist. Then I gave it another twist.

Gas Pedal was originally published years ago in a much shorter form on the UK crime fiction website *Near to the Knuckle*. My memory is a little foggy, but something tells me it's the product of a very bad mood, the type where you just want to watch the world explode into flame and rubble. This type of troubled mindset often leads people to do very bad things. Occasionally you'll see a news headline of someone who just snaps, kills some people and then kills themselves. I always wonder what goes through someone's head in those final furious moments. This story is my take on how one such person decided to go out with a bang.

The Red Card originally appeared in *Under the Bed Vol. 5, No. 5*. A mysterious threat from an unknown source struck me as an intriguing premise, and that's exactly what the red card represents when Caroline finds it in her new apartment. The plot hinges on the tension between the natural scientific world and the supernatural world, which some humans refuse to believe in … possibly at their own peril. This story earned my first piece of actual fan mail from a reader, and for that it will always remain close to my heart.

The Neighbor at the Curb came about one morning while my wife and I were rushing to get the kids ready for day care. I looked out our upstairs window while holding my youngest in my arms, and saw our neighbor rolling his garbage bin to the curb. For no particular reason, I wondered if he had anything sinister hidden in the bin. My imagination took off, and I ended up plotting the whole story from my upstairs window, storyboarding how things might realistically unfold if the neighbor across the street were to go on a crazed murder spree and attack my family at home. No humor in this one; it goes for the throat.

Jacob Mosley's Raw Deal shows what is bound to happen when someone makes a deal with the devil. The deal always comes at a high price. This story was a bit too long to find a home in an anthology or magazine, so it is presented here for the very first time. And it's got teeth.

<u>Matthew Weber's Acknowledgments</u>

I'd like to thank Shanna, Hudson, Miller and Maribeth, and anyone who has ever bothered to read my stories. I'd also like to thank in no particular order: My sister Lauren, Mom, Dad and Aunt Carol, Little Professor Books, Barron/Ritchie/Jeff/Tim from my punk rock band Skeptic?, Rance Wilbourn (medical consultant), Vic Kerry, the Sisters of Slaughter (Michelle & Melissa), Chad Lutzke, John Boden, Paula Limbaugh, Mark Matthews, Simon Dewar, Nathon Balka, Amanda Hard, J.C. Michael, K. Trap Jones, M.B. Vujacic, Patrick Freivald, Karen Runge, Lori Michelle and Critters.org.

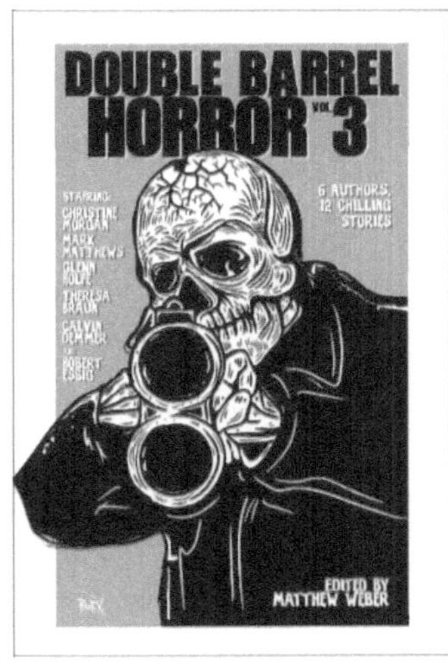